AMONG WOLVES

AMONG WOLVES

Erica Blaque

Copyright © 2022 by Erica Blaque

Cover and jacket design by 2Faced Design

ISBN: 978-1-951709-93-8

eISBN: 978-1-951709-99-0

Library of Congress Control Number: available upon request

First hardcover edition September 2022

by Polis Books, LLC

62 Ottowa Road S

Marlboro, NJ 07746

www.PolisBooks.com

POLIS BOOKS

*This novel is dedicated to the guardian I've chosen in this life,
who has never faltered in her support of my dreams;
I love you forever.
And to Cindi for modeling to a little girl that it's okay
to be different. You are incredibly missed.*

I'm angry with him because he gave up on us. I'm angry with him because he ignores me. I'm angry with him because he only does the bare minimum, yet expects everything from me. I'm angry with him because he doesn't romance me anymore, but still expects sex. I'm angry with him because he values his phone above all else.

I hate him because he treasures his career more than our marriage. I hate him because he cheats.

My husband is a self-important asshole—but he isn't a murderer.

Prologue

Brooke Sadler's fully clothed body lies on its back on the floor of her bright kitchen, her head resting on her right ear. If her heart were still beating, the pulse in her jugular would be visible in her petite neck. Rigor mortis already distorts her once beautiful, glowing flesh. Her face is kissed with sporadic flashes of light from investigators taking photos. Her fit body shows no signs of injury or trauma.

The condo is that of a young woman with modern taste. Each throw pillow placed impeccably, and each silver polished picture frame perfectly positioned. A white cat stretches its lazy legs, blending into the white area rug that spreads across much of the small living room floor.

Her elderly neighbor's tears glisten in the morning light as her hands wipe them away and she explains that she saw an unknown man leave late in the night but isn't sure of the time, only that the sun had set but not yet risen. She had awoken to voices in the hallway outside her front door, then quietly peeked through her door's peephole, stepping away from her door slowly so that her creaky floor would not give her spying away. She describes the mystery man with ease: his hair a dark and thick brown, but no facial hair. She compares him to a young Tom Selleck. She says the mystery man was quite handsome and tall, but not skinny like some tall men can be.

Brooke seems to have died a natural death. The presence of one object tells the medical examiner that Brooke's toxicology report will reveal that isn't the case.

The medical examiner wipes his forehead with a hairy forearm. He's thankful his new personal protective equipment doesn't cover them because the heat of the condo, along with the pressure to perform his duties with precision, makes his skin sticky. He wishes they could open a door or window to break the stale, hot atmosphere in the young woman's apartment. As much as his skin craves the cool morning air, they must keep the condo guarded and closed during the investigation. He slides the silver stiletto of his thermometer into Brooke's abdomen, piercing her liver to obtain her core temperature. He performs each step in his process slowly with the utmost accuracy. He knows this death will make national news.

A yelp hurts his ears and for a moment he forgets how uncomfortably hot he is. The yelp becomes a blubbering howl. The medical examiner peeks around the kitchen island, still crouched beside Brooke, to see the howling woman now lay limp in the arms of a policeman outside the front door. Her desperate cry like a pair of sharp claws being drug across the floor of a silent room. He guesses it's the broken cry of a mother who was told she lost a child. He moves back to Brooke's body as the woman demands to see her baby—her sweetheart. It won't be true unless she sees Brooke for herself.

He glances across the kitchen at the detective who waits patiently but is obviously eager to hear his initial judgments. She needs to start preparing for the press and, equally important, her boss. One body may be anonymous, might even go unnoticed by the people of a small city like Deep River. But two in the same unique way? That means the national spotlight.

The medical examiner stands, inspecting the object resting on the white marble counter that tells him Brooke was murdered—just like the other woman. This is the second time he's seen this. Megan Coldwell's house was the same: Nothing out of place. No sign of struggle. Body showing no external injuries as it lay on the kitchen floor fully clothed. Her eyes also wide open in disbelief as they watched the world around her fade slowly into nothingness.

No matter how many times he's seen death, it never grows ordinary. The way we are here one moment then gone the next: it's something that never gets easier to understand. How we only leave behind a sack of organic material that immediately begins to decompose back into the world is always humbling to him.

Her mother yelps again from outside the front door as he studies Brooke's face and ponders all the things she had and hadn't done. He thinks of everything that has gone to waste with such a young death: her first steps, her first love, learning and gaining knowledge throughout the years for it to be pointless now. He glares at the cup on the countertop with the crimson college mascot for the Washington State Cougars plastered obnoxiously large on it, a strange sensation needles him. He thinks of her as a student purchasing that mug, only to have it used as the vehicle for her murder.

"The cat," his husky voice belts out to the awkward young man above him while keeping his gaze on the cup. The assistant follows instructions and steps to the cat. He bends with his knees, hovering above the furry blob laying in a sunbeam on the living room floor. He inspects the furry body, lifting each paw, gently spreading the pink paw pads. He rolls the white blob over and carefully examines the other side. Lifting its lips, inspecting its gums. The cat lightly bats at his hand but allows the intrusion.

"Nothing," the young assistant reports.

"Keep it away," the medical examiner stresses.

The assistant scoops up the cat, reaching for its collar that reads "Fluff," causing his potbelly to bounce with a single chuckle. The cat meows a pathetic meow, announcing its annoyance, but again, allows the intrusion.

The medical examiner snaps his fingers at the photographer, demanding tighter shots of the cup resting on the white counter. He leans over it, making sure not to disturb the photographer while studying the aroma and appearance of tea. He knows the liquid is lethal.

Crouching back down to Brooke, he studies her lovely face again. Her stick-straight, silky chestnut hair drapes across the tile floor, with a few stray strands stuck to her dry, cracked lips. He wonders who she didn't see coming.

"David?" The young detective speaks softly from across the

kitchen. Her patience growing thin.

The medical examiner lifts his head above the kitchen island, making eye contact with the detective who is now perched on the opposite side of the island. "Yes, Cruz?" he responds innocently.

Her facial expression doesn't need further explaining. She needs answers, at least his initial thoughts, so she can figure out how to present them.

He answers in code, knowing she'll understand. "It's the cup," he says with a single nod at the countertop.

"Shit," Detective Cruz hisses, her dark eyes floating to the cup with the Washington State Cougars logo. She inhales sharply, then exhales slowly, allowing her full lips to balloon slightly.

"I'll hurry my report as best I can for you, sweetheart," he says, acknowledging her anxiety.

Cruz would normally take offense at "sweetheart," having fought long and hard against the stain her beauty creates on her career. But his "sweetheart" is a term of endearment; she knows he'd also use it if she were a man. "It must be done by the book, though. You and I both know this is going to be under scrutiny," he adds, knowing she'll sympathize.

Cruz moans a response; that's exactly why she needs his report as soon as possible. She marches back to the corner, her long black ponytail bouncing off her back with each step.

Detective Cruz reaches for her cellphone in her suit pocket, the vibration alerting her to a phone call. The display lights up with a photograph of her partner, Trent Valletta.

"Yeah?" Detective Cruz says sharply into her phone.

"Is it the same?" he asks in Spanish.

"Yeah," confirming their suspicion.

His long and loud exhale matches her feelings.

"I'll see you later?" is both a question and a statement after a long silence.

"Yeah," she rasps before ending the call.

Detective Cruz continues observing quietly, staying still as a hunter eyeing its prey. Her brain retrieves facts as her instinct creates connections between the invisible dots.

Fifty-four percent of women are killed by someone they knew.

The detective watches the bodies move through the apartment, each doing a specific and important task. Her eyes glance at the two access points again: no forcible entry, no visible struggle.

Brooke knew her killer.

It's time to find the mystery man the neighbor saw.

1

The Death of Love

When does love die, exactly? Is it when one person stops trying, or does one stop trying because they've fallen out of love? I believe Rob loves me dearly; he loves my face, my body, my grace, and my ability to fit into any social situation he tosses me in. It's true, I fit perfectly into the life of a man like him.

I stroll by the room in our house that is his dedicated home office, wearing my favorite black leggings and a sweater that is his. I stop for a moment to glance at him hovered over his keyboard as he pounds away at the keys. His firm bare chest lit up by the electronic glow of the dual monitors. I take a sip of my tea, studying his large feet tucked under the desk that wiggle while he forms his next thought. He sees me and lifts his head to offer a loving smile.

"Almost done," he says again. The last time I checked on him was thirty minutes ago and he said the same thing. I'll probably crawl into bed alone tonight.

When we first began dating, Rob and I made love a few times a day. His scent, his breath, the way he smelled while taking me were all so intoxicating. I couldn't get enough, and neither could he. We still make love a few times a week when he isn't traveling for work, but it isn't the same. The motions are there, the moves are the same, but he isn't *there* there. Not like he used to be.

Before I walk away to place my empty cup in the sink, I catch him check his cellphone and crack a suggestive smile. A smile that threatens to make my upper lip curl.

I've caught him cheating three times. Red-handed. Guilt-stricken.

The first time was with a woman who worked at Anexa, his pharmaceutical management and research company. Her name was Joy. She doesn't get a last name and she sure as hell didn't bring any joy, at least not to me. She sent a nude photo to his cellphone that I also received on our iPad. I could see the whole text conversation. It went something like this.

*Joy: *Nude selfie of her standing in front of a mirror. Fake breasts. Fake tan. Fake blonde. Fake nails. Zero pubic hair. **

Rob: Jesus. (insert some stupid emoji here)

Joy: Busy tonight? I miss you.

Rob: Not. At. All. When and where?

Joy: My place again. Let's say 9?

Rob: See you then, sexy.

I sat in our kitchen reading this brief but world-destroying conversation. I'll always remember the feeling of my trembling limbs, my stomach threatening to fall out of me, time slowing, and my chest growing too dense to stand.

It's silly, really. The cliché I became at that very moment. The college-educated woman who quit her job as a respected project manager to be a stay-at-home mom. A woman with a wildly successful husband to care for her and her yet-to-be offspring. I hated myself more than I hated him for letting myself get into such a situation. I've never understood how women say they never saw it coming—until I didn't. I thought we were happy, in love, and amazing together in bed. I thought we were what everyone wanted to be. Apparently—unbeknownst to me—we were not.

I confronted him when he entered the kitchen to lie to me, to tell me he had work he must tend to at Anexa's nearly completed campus. To be honest, I can't remember the impressively detailed lie he devised. I cried. I screamed. I threw things. He had never heard me yell until that night.

And what did he say? What they always say. He was sorry, and it would never happen again.

I gently set my empty cup in the sink before flicking off each light as I make my way back to his office to kiss him goodnight. Before I reach him, still sitting at his enormous wooden desk I picked for this space, he quickly flips his phone over so that the screen is facing down. I grip his muscular shoulders from behind then lean around him to kiss his cheek that is dusted with thorny black hair.

"Love you," he whispers with his British accent that still has that ability to catch me off guard in the best way. "Good night," he says without taking his eyes from the monitor where he has already written a few hundred words. The other monitor filled with news showing the nation-wide protests and rioting. I stand for a moment, watching Americans who are angry with their government swarm the streets of Seattle, marching and reciting the same chant in unison. The protests are growing quickly, even here in the small conservative city of Deep River.

I walk away, tightening his large sweater around my torso as I turn to see him shamelessly reach for his phone again, triggering queasiness to vibrate my stomach and my chest to grow heavy.

The second time I caught him cheating, he was at a conference in Miami where I flew to surprise him. However, it was I who received the surprise when I walked in on him inside a twenty-something "Instagram model." She fit the same bill as the other with fake everything and a tiny waist. I don't remember her face or even the expression on his. I just remember her tacky, acrylic shoes; they were still on her as she rode my husband. That time I was more offended by his choice. Here I am, Jackie fucking Kennedy, and he wants to screw all the cheap wannabe Marilyns.

He found me at the Miami airport and, again, promised it would never happen again. He even shed a few tears that time. It was so believable, I swear.

"Sophia. I don't know what's wrong with me. I'm sorry. Please. I'll die if you leave."

After washing my face and brushing my teeth, I strip down to nothing before crawling into my pre-warmed bed. The heat slowly envelops my bare skin as I pull the thick down comforter over my naked body. The night is black, with no moon to illuminate it. The only light seeping through the blackness comes from the soft light in Rob's office, creeping into our bedroom from down the hallway. I reach for my cellphone and scroll through my Facebook feed from under the warmth of my bedding. After various news articles and photographs of the streets crowded with protesters, happy news breaks through the chaos. A smiling woman stands belly-to-belly with her balding husband, both holding a sonogram between them. I've sat with her at charity luncheons, so I know this pregnancy isn't her first. She has many little ones with her fat husband. Her photo shoves my mind into resentment, clouding it with complex jealousy.

I wanted children. I wanted a large family. We talked of our dreams, and children were intertwined into the fabric of what our life together was supposed to be.

Rob was raised in a borough of London named Chelsea. He's the only child of a well-off and well-known family in that area. He grew up having everything and consumes as if he never has enough. Looking back, I see now that he spoke of our future children as if they were titles to display, or even phases all people must endure. He never had the desire for children like I did. He wanted to display the photograph of our little Robert Charles Claire II, but I wanted to raise him, love him, and teach him. I wanted to watch him grow into an intelligent, loving, and kind man.

I never got my Robert Charles Claire II, or any other children. After a year of trying for a baby, we went to a fertility specialist and were tested for abnormalities. Apparently, my husband is sterile due to a sexually transmitted disease that had gone undetected for too long. Yes, I had it, too. We were both treated, and it was like nothing had happened, but it did because I can't have children with my husband. We could adopt, but he frowns upon that, as does his family, and I crave my own flesh and blood.

After that, I threw myself into charity work and various organizations. I'm on several boards and have raised more money than most make in a lifetime. I raise money for several organizations: funding research for cancer, fighting for human rights, and feeding the hungry. I've also remodeled our home twice because my desire to plan projects never went away after quitting my job as a project manager.

I set my phone down on the charging dock on my nightstand, then kick one foot out from under the heavy down comforter. My mind drifts effortlessly towards sleep until worry sneaks its way in, stopping the craved release. Besides my husband, my younger sister is always at the forefront of my burdensome worry.

Cassidy, who is always in need of some support, particularly after breaking up with the most recent loser she was dating, sails into my head. Her boyfriend's range in incompetence, but most are unemployed, abusive sociopaths. One boyfriend, Angelo, beat her so badly that he put her in the hospital. Our parents paid her hospital bill, then moved her in with them. Cassidy always needs saving, and caring for her is now my job since our parents died together in a car accident caused by a drunk driver.

Sleep finally wins, edging slowly over the anxiety. The euphoric release I crave begins to take me when a high-pitch siren blasts through the bedroom, blaring off each wall, tearing into my eardrums. Rob storms into our bedroom, flicking the light on, causing me to squint at him as I try to make sense of what's happening. He's yelling at me, but I can't make out his words over the shrieking siren. He moves quickly, his body now standing at my side of the bed where I still lay, propped up on my elbows. He rips the thick down comforter off the bed and scoops me up in it, rushing me out of our bedroom in his arms.

I swallow hard, but my throat is uncomfortably tight, making it difficult. "Rob, what's happening?" I ask with my arms around his neck and my lips to his ear. Our burglar alarm continues piercing deep into my ears. Rob stops abruptly, dropping me onto my feet, then shoves me into his office and yells in my ear to lock the door behind him. As he rushes from his office, I reach out from under the heavy blanket wrapped around my naked body and lock his office door.

The siren stops after a few moments. A strange white-noise fills my ears—a residue left from the loud siren. I readjust the large blanket to cover my body completely. My bare feet grow heavy and cold on the dark wood floor as I stare at the doorknob, waiting to hear any noise from Rob, but none comes. The sound of my heart pounding competes with the white noise ringing in my ears. Time slows to a crawl as I wait to hear Rob's voice from the other side of the large wooden door.

I will my legs to move, but the adrenaline has frozen them. My pounding heart now deafening.

Willing my body to move, I turn around swiftly and begin scanning his office for a way to call for help, but I only see his computer, which has a lock code I don't know. I step towards the desk, hoping to see his cellphone, which would allow me to make an emergency call without knowing the code. I notice a silver pin sitting on his desk. The pin is made up of a pyramid that's created with one thick continuous silver line, with another thick continuous line creating an infinity symbol running vertical through the pyramid.

I reach my hand out from under the down comforter. Stretching for the pin, I trip on the blanket bunching at my feet.

I catch my balance, and that's when I see it: two eyes watching me through the oversized window behind Rob's desk. The white of the eyeballs stand out more than anything else. My limbs freeze again as my eyes focus with incredible sharpness on the owner of the eyes. Just as fast as I saw the two eyes watching me, they disappear.

"Rob!" I scream, running for his office door and unlocking it with haste. I sail through the doorway, glancing back at the window, as the side of my face crashes into Rob's bare chest. He catches me in his strong arms, squeezing me.

"What is it?" Robs asks, cradling my head to his chest. "Sophia, what happened?" Rob holds me tightly, frantically searching over the top of my head for the reason of my scream.

"There was someone there. I saw eyes watching me." I point at the window from the safety of Rob's arms.

"I saw him, too. The police are on their way," Rob announces. "Who was that?"

"I don't know, my love," his British accent thicker from the adrenaline as he hisses, "fucking nerve."

As the police question us and inspect the property and camera footage, I silently question how Rob knew it was a man.

As far as I could see, it could have been a woman. My doubt caused by his past actions creates a thick suspicion that the prowler was not a man, but instead a woman.

The third time I caught Rob cheating, I didn't say anything because I technically didn't catch him. I found him on a dating site for married people. I also didn't say anything because, at this point, what is there to say? After all, the world is a far too volatile place to be at war with what should be my most important ally.

I still believe he can change. I know, silly me. But if he doesn't, I'll go mad.

2

A Peaceful Death

I wear an all-white cotton nightgown—something my grandmother might have worn to bed with her stringy grey hair hanging to her waist. Its thickness covering my arms and hanging off my shoulders all the way down to my ankles. I walk barefoot on the rooftop of a tall building through the night's sky with city lights glowing beneath me like a dull candle from across the room. A stiff breeze that I cannot feel—neither warm nor cold—pressing my nightgown against my body.

Meeting the edge of the roof, my toes curl over the edge. The breeze now a light wind whipping my long brown hair around my face and nightgown-covered shoulders. I grasp the cross dangling from a chain around my neck with my right hand, my mother's cross. My hand tightens into a fist around it. I glance down at the unfamiliar city street below. Someone is behind me, their wickedness palpable and their sin unmistakably familiar.

I swivel on my heels, careful not to test my balance on the edge, meeting the eyes of the wicked one just as my alarm rattles my mind out of the dream. The dream that started when the murders did, allowing me to only see a few moments at a time. Like with all dreams, the feeling involved is more important than the actions. The feeling attached to this dream is that of guilty relief. As if hearing a loved one was not on a plane that crashed, closely followed by the hollow sadness for the people who did have a loved one in the crash that left no survivors.

I reach for my phone, turning off my alarm, then lay in bed for a moment longer, taking in the day ahead. The sun hasn't risen, yet it kisses the world with a dull grey light, growing brighter with each passing moment. The world at dawn offers a special calmness. The sense of the day ahead and all the hope it offers fills me with positivity as I throw my robe around my bare shoulders and tie it tightly around my waist. I begin the trek to the kitchen, with my right hand squeezing tightly around my mother's cross.

As the sun slowly peaks, the dry flat landscape of Deep River appears like an oil painting. The Columbia River bending through the middle of it like a streamer falling freely to the ground. The city will vibrate intensely soon with everyone readying themselves for their Monday, turning I-82 into a slow-moving snake of red lights.

My phone vibrates on the stone kitchen counter, causing me to reach for it instinctively, but I fight the urge. I need just one more moment to myself, gazing out over Deep River from the comfort of my kitchen while enjoying my morning coffee. Last night's terrifying intrusion feels as if it was a dream muddled in with my actual dream, but my lingering restlessness assures me it wasn't. The eyes that watched me through Rob's home office window still feel as if they are on me. Their glare poring over my skin, studying my movements. Shadows seem to dance in the corner of my eyesight, and the silence of our home I once cherished is now unnerving.

Glancing out the window to our nearest neighbor, I watch their new car inch down their long driveway, then slowly pull onto the neighborhood street. While we have much space between us, the lack of year-round, thick green trees makes me thankful I pushed to have privacy film placed on our windows. Not only for privacy, but the windows take in the intense morning sun. It seems any trees in Deep River are planted by man and must be treated with care to survive the brutal winters and hateful summers.

Rob will be home soon from the gym and he'll ask if I want to take a shower with him. I'll probably say yes.

My phone vibrates again. I'm compelled to check it, to make sure it's not Rob in need. Instead, I see it's Melanie. A woman who would call me her friend. She's the perpetual gossiper. Always has the latest news about people, events, or places. I believe she missed her calling as a tacky tabloid reporter, but she also fits nicely into her role as an unsatisfied housewife. I glance long enough at the text for it to pique my interest.

OMG. Did you see the news?

I open the text and see her extreme usage of emojis and a link. The link directs me to the *Deep River Herald*, our local newspaper. The headline reads, "Another Woman Found Dead. Community Fears for Its Safety."

I've followed the media's creation of this story and it has grown larger than I thought it would. I guess I should have anticipated such a reaction in such a small city like Deep River. This story now has its own pulse, right alongside the protesting.

Opening the article, I begin to read the scarce details the police are offering. But even the little details offered cause the hairs on my arms to stand.

"Sophia, my love!" His cheerful voice startles me.

"Geez, you scared me!" I say, slightly annoyed at Rob, who strides into the kitchen dressed in gym shorts and a t-shirt from a charity event his company held last year.

"Sorry, beautiful. Why so tense?" He tosses his keys onto the counter where my phone just was.

"I was just reading about another woman they found," I say, still holding my phone in my hand, scanning the digital words of the article.

"Another?"

"Yeah. They still don't have any leads, the article says." I set my phone down and reach for my coffee cup, still steaming with tasty warmth.

"That's alarming." His tone implies he's already bored with our conversation.

"Yes," I say, shifting my eyes to him, watching him mix his post-workout shake. His arm muscles tight and defined from the abuse they've taken at the gym.

"Do you know what fentanyl is?" I ask before taking another sip of my coffee.

"Of course, it's used in anesthesia for severe pain."

"Oh, did you know that's how the two women died?"

He ignores my follow-up question, but offers, "It's dangerous and has a reputation for dependency. It's roughly eighty times stronger than morphine and forty times more potent than heroin." He raises an eyebrow at me.

"Wow," I say to appease his ego. "They say the women didn't feel anything. Is that true?"

"Yes, that is most likely true. In their case, it probably brought unconsciousness, then complete respiratory arrest."

I glance out the large windows of my dining area overlooking Deep River, taking in the treeless hills that still somehow turn color with the changing seasons. I close my eyes, envisioning the mechanics of the drug while spinning my wedding ring in circles with the tip of my thumb. I ask with my eyes closed tightly, "So…they fell asleep…their lungs stopped working, and then their heart stopped beating. Eventually, they are brain dead," I finish, then open my eyes to see Rob's stare locked on me.

"In about six minutes. Yes," he answers, then finishes the last of his shake in one hard gulp.

"Huh," I say, still picturing the drug's effect on the organic material of the human body.

"Why?" He chuckles at my morbid line of questioning. "They died peacefully," he assures me while placing his empty cup in the sink for me or the housekeeper to place in the dishwasher that's only a foot away from the sink.

I smile when he kisses the back of my head, pushing it slightly forward. He squeezes my shoulders and instead of an injection of comfort, it hardens my muscles. He leans around me and kisses my cheek, expecting me to turn to meet his lips. When I don't, he uses his hand to twist my chin to meet his, then presses his lips softly to mine. He breaks from my lips, staying in front of my face, and offers a welcoming smile. "Shower?" he asks.

"Sure."

We make love in the shower, and before he leaves, he tells me how lucky he is to have me. I watch him—my husband, an impressive man in many ways—drive away in his new silver Audi as a twinge of gloom gnaws at me.

Padding down the hallway, I enter our bright bathroom to get ready for my carefully planned day. I use my cellphone to turn the TV on in my mirror. The white marbled floor warms my feet from the heated units that automatically turned on earlier this morning.

In the shower, I stand for minutes, letting the warm water stream down the goosebumps protruding from my naked skin, creating a prickly sensation when combined with the cool air sneaking in. While washing myself of Rob, I continue to ponder the drug used in the murders and the body's reaction to it.

While drying my hair and styling it, I mentally organize my day and how to manage my time: I have the charity ball to finish planning and a board meeting for SafeSpot, a nonprofit intended to help local homeless youth.

After my phone dings, I glance down at the screen, alerting me to a post I've been tagged in on Facebook. I wipe any residual makeup from my fingers, then glide through the device to open the Facebook app. Viewing the notification, I see it's an advertisement for the upcoming charity ball I'm planning. When I swipe back to my newsfeed, preparing to close the app, a photo generates a tension in me that mutes the world around me. The picture shows Rob sitting at an eight-top table covered in white linen. The post states it's a luncheon for Anexa. The sea of tables behind him are filled with bodies, each person casually enjoying the companionship of others while eating their lunch.

Rob sits at the table, hunched over his long legs from a belly laugh. His face tight in an honest smile. A curvy, black-haired beauty sitting next to him has her manicured brown hand resting high on his thigh while leaning into him, joining in on the laughter. It appears she is the reason he is laughing.

No one else might notice the familiarity of her touch and their body language, but seeing a woman that comfortable with my husband burns my cheeks a bright pink. Time slows as I study her before I see she is tagged in the photo. My stomach shudders, warning me not to proceed, but the all-consuming need to know pushes me forward.

I click on the woman's Facebook profile to investigate. Her name is Rosey Franklin and her glamorous beauty instantly makes me bitter. Her profile picture is suggestive as her red lips pucker for the camera with one of her chocolate-colored eyes closed in a flirty wink. Her private Facebook page only shows select information, but what I can see of her page, it promotes that she is a real estate agent, and her relationship status is "It's Complicated."

I eagerly scroll through photos that are not private, even though there is no reason for me to do so, as it only causes my stomach to flip. A discomfort that is now molding into anger and disgust. The world around me continues to be muted, with nothing else mattering but the next photo I can access. I slide rapidly from one photo to the next, reading each caption, quickly studying anyone who is tagged.

I stop at a photo of her in Atlanta from two months ago that freezes time. My gut tells me there is something distinctive about this photo. In the photo, she is wearing skintight jeans that hug her curves and a plunging V-neck white bodysuit. Her black hair is curled and allowed to fall freely to her remarkably tiny waist as she poses in front of a statue alone. She is, again, winking at the camera. The comments are full of men digitally catcalling, and girlfriends asking why she was alone in Atlanta. Her responses are vague, but she mentions in one reply that she would explain later.

No need to explain. Rob was in Atlanta at the same time.

The TV in my vanity mirror booms the local news, forcing my eyes away from the picture of Rosey taken in Atlanta—mostly likely by my husband. With my phone still frozen in my now sweaty hand, I watch the TV, where in a sea of reporters and cameramen, a single reporter is questioning a young detective. She is stunningly beautiful, Latina, and petite. Her black hair slicked back into a tight, low ponytail that hangs to her mid-back. Her grey, loose-fitting suit is obviously trying to hide her petite frame. Everything about her is a sorry attempt to hide her beauty in an industry where beauty is a weakness.

Reporter: "Do you believe this is the same person…is there a killer on the loose?"

Detective: "This is an active investigation."

Reporter: "Did this woman die similarly to the other?"

Detective: "Yes. Death was by fentanyl overdose."
Reporter: "Are there signs of sexual assault?"
Detective: "We are investigating."
Reporter: "Do the police have any suspects?"
Detective: "We will—"

The detective is interrupted by another question from another reporter eager to get his question heard. She turns away sharply from the reporters, causing her ponytail to sail in the air behind her, then walks away from the rowdy crowd with her shoulders tucked tightly back and her head held high. Being interrupted is a deal breaker for her. She intrigues me.

"I like her," I say out loud, smirking at the television before glancing back down at my phone still resting in my hand, displaying the picture of Rosey Franklin winking at me. I quickly back out of her profile, then clear my history on Facebook, and then on Google just to be safe.

The TV shows the sea of reporters yelling their questions over one another at the empty podium where the beautiful detective was.

A photograph of the recent victim appears on the screen. Her name is Brooke Sadler, and her American beauty is unmistakable. In the photo, she reveals an infectious and kind smile, showcasing her perfect teeth and dimples as she rests her hands on her waist that is left bare by a crop top. A graphic on the top corner of the screen displays a website where people can provide donations to help her family with burial services. The reporter begins to explain who she was—you know, the usual: loved, someone's daughter, someone's sister, a hard worker, college student with hopes and dreams. The reporter announces that her former employer is willing to match any donations, which sounds like something I'd suggest to Rob for positive community involvement. The reporter states the name of her employer, Anexa. Rob would have to approve such a public donation. Why did he act surprised when I told him about Brooke's death? My body freezes and my throat opens, preparing for vomit.

3

Painkiller

I've always loved the science behind what my husband's company does. Science was my favorite topic in school, and it still fascinates me. Microbiology is simply incredible; watching life we cannot normally see with the help of a microscope. Or learning about miraculous organic composition, physical chemical systems and processes is a simple thrill. Watching matter react as if it were carefully planned to do so. Chemical reactions are their own little projects being planned and executed, landing in exact, predictable measurements. It's something to be admired.

While Rob and I eat lunch together in his office, provided by the head chef of the employee kitchen, he mentions Fred, his director of policy at Trimble Laboratory, is working on something I'd find interesting. I smile as I chew, "I'll stop by," I manage after rushing to swallow.

I notice our local newspaper on his desk, the *Deep River Herald*. The front page displaying a photograph of a middle-aged woman holding a white sign that reads in red and blue marker, "No Justice. No Peace." The Deep River city center is behind her, with a sea of others holding signs or raising their fist at the tall building their officials occupy. The people are not happy with their government for many reasons.

"The police must have their hands full right now," I say, nodding to the newspaper on his desk.

He keeps his gaze on his plate of baked salmon and steamed broccoli, missing my nod at the newspaper. He responds, "Yeah, the murders seem to be taking up a large portion of their time when the streets are running rampant with liberals. You'd think they'd have jobs they should be at instead of protesting," he scoffs before shoving another forkful of baked salmon into his mouth. "Maybe they ought to stick to their territory of government handouts." His British accent sounding out "territory" like tear-it-tree through a full mouth.

I don't correct him, but squint in curiosity at his assumption of my meaning. We've never met eye-to-eye on politics and I wasn't starting another debate of democrats against republicans, especially in his office.

Rob glances at his watch. "My love, I have a meeting starting in two." That is my prompt to leave, never mind that I'm not finished with my salad.

I gather our dishes, placing them on the table in the corner of his office for the dining staff to retrieve.

"Hello, gentlemen. How's the weather in the beautiful Hawkeye State?" Rob smiles at his computer monitor as various male voices fumble over one another before they fall silent, allowing one voice to answer.

Reaching for my purse, I glance at his monitor displaying six men in suits sitting at a table, all ready to answer Rob's questions. I blow Rob a silent kiss that goes unnoticed as I step out of his office, shutting the door quietly.

As promised, I stroll into the Trimble Laboratories on Anexa's campus. Then, with a wave of Rob's badge, I walk through the large security door to Fred's office, which really isn't an office, more like his informal designated area in the large lab he manages. I pass two stations, watching each face study what's in their microscopes intently. I see Fred ahead, his dark skin contrasting against his white lab coat. The white room seems to place him on display. He lifts his head from the paperwork resting in his hands to meet my gaze, and smiles with knowing warmth.

"Sophia!" he shouts joyfully from across the big white room. His voice loud enough for everyone to glance in his direction, then mine.

Instead of shouting in return, I offer a large smile and quicken my pace towards him, causing my Rene Caovilla stiletto booties to clack louder.

"Hi, Fred!" I set my handbag down on a chair near him then reach for a hug. He quickly squeezes me in return, but his age betrays his ability to squeeze tightly.

"Oh, Sophia, what have I done to deserve this visit today?" His wrinkled and freckled hands reach for mine, cupping one within both of his. His hands are cold and boney, and his scent of aged books fills the air around him.

"Rob mentioned you were working on something pretty amazing and, well, you know me," I sheepishly say, shrugging my shoulders.

"Oh boy, do I. Forever curious, my young Sophia!" he says as he turns to place his paperwork into a silver wire tray labeled *Trial C-M110508*. "Come, come," he says, signaling for me to follow him as he shuffles away. "All this fuss in the streets reminds me of the 1960s!" he says, his voice hollow and breathy as he refers to the protesters at the city center.

"Now I know you were disappointed you couldn't look at what I was working on last time, but it was too dangerous for you. I couldn't risk you being exposed to pathogens. This, though," he gleams with enthusiasm and shakes his index finger in the air, "this you can enjoy, my curious Sophia." He stops at a workstation where three employees hover over one microscope sealed in a glovebox, all joined in a stiff group discussion. They raise their heads in unison to meet Fred, ignoring my presence. I wonder if they know who I am. The wife of their boss's boss. I doubt they'd care if they knew, though. I've noticed that the scientists at Rob's companies care little for those like me; those who didn't "earn" their title. They only recognize accolades granted on intellectual merit.

"May I?" Fred asks his subordinates, who then scatter throughout the laboratory, leaving their work in the glovebox.

"This, my curious Sophia, is one of the things we are working on that is very exciting!" His milky brown eyes light up under his thick glasses. Fred is years past retirement age, but he loves what he does, and he enjoys teaching. He is someone my husband is happy to keep around for as long as he can. Rob is lucky to have him; his intellect has made Rob a lot of money.

Rob has always been great at hiring people smarter than he. He knows where to place people, and how to utilize them.

Fred snaps on gloves and places protective glasses over his prescription glasses. He then inserts his hands into the thick glovebox gloves. He carefully and slowly removes the petri dish the employees were gazing at under the microscope, placing a new one on the microscope's stage. His bony hand tremors slightly as he precisely measures a white powder, pouring it into the petri dish with ease.

He gestures for me to step closer as he hands me safety glasses.

"What is it, exactly?" I ask him as he reaches for a pre-filled syringe resting on a metal plate within the glovebox.

"The biological effects of this potent compound are similar to morphine. It binds to the protein in plasma." He licks his lips as he presses his safety glasses against the eyepieces to the microscope.

"What is it?" I ask again, leaning closer with obvious interest.

"We're going to fluctuate the pH in this fentanyl hybrid in an attempt to find a sweet spot for the distribution of the fentanyl to the central nervous system." He lifts only his head, staying leaned over the glovebox, his face directed at me. "Would you care to look, young lady?" He asks the question with a teasing smile, already knowing the answer.

I smile big, nodding my head quickly.

"So why alter the drug if it already does what it's supposed to?"

"Well, it is an amazing drug for pain management, but we

are trying to change its pharmacological effects to better target specific pain."

I rest the safety glasses on my nose, then lean over the microscope eyepieces, holding my hands tightly behind my back as Fred adjusts the fine adjustment knob.

My mouth releases a confused gasp as I watch the structure of the matter change before my eyes as Fred adds a clear liquid to the powder. The little girl in me is giddy with excitement.

"Sophia?"

I straighten my spine to meet Fred's questioning eyes, still wearing the thick, clear safety glasses.

"Have you been keeping safe with the…what's happened around here lately?"

"The murders in Deep River?" I say the words he would rather not use.

His frail body shifts on his heels. "Yes."

"Well, yes. You know me," I say as I remove the glasses and set them softly on the solid metal counter.

"Yes, I do. Infinitely curious." He smiles, as if saying I'm too curious for my own good, and I offer a smile in return. "When you would come into the lab with Benjamin, before he…left, I could tell how much you loved learning. You absorb information quickly, grasshopper," he says, giggling at his own silliness. I offer a tight grin in return, but the thought of Benjamin Booth and I here in what was once his laboratory presses heavily on my chest. My mind fills with him: the euphoria his touch sent through my body, the sound of his voice snug to my ear, his smile so similar to my husband's but warmer. But then the sadness quickly surfaces, causing my heart—my poor heart—

to grow painfully void.

Ben and I would spend long hours here, playing with the toys that Trimble Laboratories has to offer. He was a composed teacher; he treasured watching my face light up as he taught me. The more he taught me, the more interested I became. This room was a secret place that was "ours." No one knew what we were to each other. I was simply the nosey wife of the boss and Ben—the director of policy—was showing me a kindness, just as Fred does now.

Fred removes the dish we were analyzing, setting it aside, then retrieves another with fresh white powder in it. "This, my dear, is a *very* special kind of fentanyl citrate. This is *ours*," he says as he places the dish under the microscope lens.

"What do you mean 'ours'?"

"Well," he fiddles with the microscope's settings, "this has a special indicator in its formulation that we—Trimble—placed into its compound." He mumbles to himself as he fidgets with the settings, watching through the eyepieces.

I put the safety glasses back on, then lean over the microscope to watch again as the mixture displays a newly formed composition as he squeezes a liquid to blend with the powder.

"Wow!" I say as I rise to meet his eyes that are suddenly filled with worry. "What is it, Fred?" I ask, concerned.

He slowly takes off the gloves and safety glasses. "Well, young lady, a vial of this particular formula went missing. It's not much, not at all. Only a tiny vial, smaller than a tube of lipstick. I was worried a competitor had gotten its hands on it. You know that's an issue here," he clears his throat, "so I reported it directly to Robert, suspecting some sort of corporate espionage after the Benjamin incident. He thanked me and...I wanted him to handle it the way he deemed fit. This was against protocol—going straight to him— but I assumed it was a competitor who stole it, but now..." He grows quiet, hanging his head with the guilt of creating a drug that is potentially being used in killing women of Deep River.

"What is it?" I move closer to him, placing my hand on his hand, using my free hand to remove the safety glasses from my face.

"That amount can do great harm, Sophia," he says, his eyes heavy with worry. "Only a fraction of that particular formula has the ability to kill someone. Fentanyl is already so strong... but that formula, my formula..." He shakes his head, indicating the potency of his creation.

"You're worried this could be the drug used in the murders?" My mind blazes an immediate road to Rob. Has Rob connected the potential for this to be the drug used in the murders just as Fred has? Rob and I discussed fentanyl; he knows it's what was used to kill both women.

"It was only a small amount taken, but enough that I would notice." One corner of his mouth turns up at the well-organized laboratory he runs.

"Rob said the women who died didn't feel anything. Is this true?" I ask, worry hanging from my brows.

"Well, yes, that is true," he says, nimbly patting the top of my hand still resting on top of his. "You see, this drug binds to the opioid receptors at a rapid rate—it's quite amazing!" Fred answers, his scientist mind working quickly to answer me in terms I'd understand. "You see, when these receptors are activated at such a rate, they can suppress the body's ability to regulate even the simplest, most automatic things—the lungs, for example. But the most dangerous part of *this* drug is its ability to pass the blood-brain barrier at an almost-instant pace. There are various side effects when used appropriately, but when an overdose occurs, it all happens too quickly. The effects happen too swiftly for the body to process."

"It's the lungs that stop working that causes death?" I ask, still curious.

"Yes, precisely. Dizziness occurs almost immediately, disorientation, then fainting. Once the body has lost consciousness, then the cessation of breathing occurs, which, in turn, obstructs all other vital organs from behaving routinely."

"How long, exactly, does it take to do that?"

"Well, that would depend on the amount and the way in which it was administered. However, even a drop, when taken orally, can cause an overdose in under one minute."

"So, if this was the drug used in the murders, would you be able to tell by the victim's blood?"

Like light riding a rail, the answer strikes him, igniting his milky eyes with awareness before he says, "Maybe not the blood, but definitely the liquid it was delivered in."

4

Savior's Arrival

Arriving home as I drive up my coiled driveway, I see an unfamiliar dark blue Ford Focus parked in front of my garage. The dark windows of the car match its blackened rims. The sun's glare stings my eyes, hindering my ability to see who is standing near the unknown car. I see a small frame leaning against the Ford Focus with arms crossed, and another bulky frame standing erect with purpose. I reach up to press my garage door button, then flip my visor down to block the sun. I recognize one of the faces: petite, beautiful, Latina. It's the detective from television.

My stomach sinks down into my pelvis instantly. It's the type of guilt that edges in when I'm pulled over for speeding, as if I'm being scolded by society's parents. I pull into my garage and step out of my car. The female detective meets me at the entrance to the opened garage door.

With the large garage door hanging over our heads, I ask, "Can I help you?"

"Are you Sophia Claire?" Her voice is raspier than it was on television, but her beauty is even more evident in person. Her overly large grey pant suit swallows her petite frame, making her look harmless. I notice her imperfect complexion for the first time. On another, the tiny skin-colored scars speckled unevenly would have taken away from their beauty.

"Yes," I answer.

"Your husband is Robert Charles Claire?" she asks, removing her sunglasses from her face and resting them on top of her head.

"Yes."

"I'm Detective Cruz with the Deep River Police Department," she flaunts her badge with pride, "and this is Detective Valletta." She nods at the bulky man still standing near their car. "We have a few questions we'd like to ask you."

"Questions? Is my husband okay?" My mind skips to Rob and my heart flutters in my chest thinking something might have happened to him.

"I believe so. I'm just here to talk," she only half assures me.

"Is this about the trespasser the other night?" I ask, squinting into the sun.

"No, I'm unaware of a trespasser. I just have a few questions."

Worry seeps throughout my muscles, creating instant fatigue.

"It will only take a minute," she pushes. The corner of her bottom lip disappears into her mouth as she waits for my answer.

"Yes, of course. I'll meet you at the front door."

She nods, backing away as I reach for the button to close the garage door. Before the door closes, I see her motion to the enormous man near the car to follow her. I walk with my Tom Ford stilettos giving away my location through the house, quickly making my way to the front door to greet her and the giant.

"Please. Come in," I say, the natural hostess in me shines.

"Thank you."

I gesture for them to choose a seat in the sitting room that overlooks our front courtyard and Deep River. The small trees in our yard are now almost stripped bare thanks to the wind. My green lawn is littered with their moist golden yellow, brown, and brilliant red leaves. With our home nestled snugly against a large treeless mountain, overlooking the neighborhood below us, I have the perfect vantage point to view the beauty of autumn.

I offer both detectives a beverage before entering the sitting room, but both decline.

Detective Cruz sits on the largest couch in the room, then reaches into her coat, pulling out a small notebook and a pen. Valletta stands next to her with his arms crossed tightly in front of his massive chest, their muscles protruding from under his short sleeve shirt. After glancing around the room, he rests his hard gaze on me, standing with his feet spread wide.

I sit next to Detective Cruz, crossing my legs immediately. We share the large couch, but I feel too close, so I wiggle away, then attempt to swallow the golf ball in my throat. I reach for my mother's cross resting on my chest, sliding the clasp to the back of my neck.

"What can I do for you?" I ask politely with my clammy hands resting in my lap.

The seven-and-a-half-foot-tall grandfather clock that stands looming in the hallway chimes 4:00 p.m. Its chiming echoes off the walls of the sitting room. We both pause as the noise continues, patiently waiting for each chime to be the last.

"Well, as I stated, I'm Detective Cruz with—"

"I know who you are. I saw you on television," I assure her.

Cruz pauses for a moment. "Then you know I'm the lead investigator of the murders of the women in the Deep River?"

I nod with a polite smile, nervously fidgeting with my wedding ring, thumbing at it violently, allowing it to dig painfully deep under my thumbnail.

"We have reason to believe that…" She stops to observe me for a moment, the corner of her pink bottom lip disappears into her mouth again as she thinks. "This isn't going to be easy to hear, Mrs. Claire. We have reason to believe that your husband has had romantic relationships with the two women who've been murdered."

There's the feeling again. It's the same every time—never dulls. My body trembles, my stomach threatens to fall out of me, time slows, and my heart breaks more. My head drops.

"Mrs. Claire?" she says softly to get my attention. I quickly lift my head to meet her gaze and offer a polite smile. "I know this isn't easy to hear."

"Do you?" I bite at her without warning. "Have you ever had your heart broken by the man you love?" My voice falters with threatening tears.

"Well, no." She glances down at her hands. I look at her hands, too, and see no ring.

"You're not married, are you?"

She shakes her head.

"Then you don't know."

"Marriage isn't for me," she offers. "I can imagine, though. And with that, I can extend sympathy."

I force another polite smile; my mother's voice reminding me that it is Godly to show true beauty through humility.

She adjusts her suit jacket while clearing her throat to speak. The woman in front of me isn't the strong commander I saw on TV. She is nervous and soft, dancing around words with compassion. She begins to speak again, her words falling hastily from her round mouth. Her delicate hands fidget with her notebook as her dark eyes scan my face.

I glance up at Detective Valletta, whose eyes haven't left me. Our eyes connect, and I hold the connection with his hard gaze while she speaks.

"...do you understand? Can you tell me where your husband was the night of the eighteenth? There was a man seen leaving Brooke Sadler's condo who looked like your husband, and drove a car matching his silver Audi."

My eyes leave the mountain of a man and settle on her dainty face. Her eyes fall to my lips, then down to my hands resting in my lap. She edges closer to me.

"Mrs. Claire?" Her cold hand lightly touches mine, removing me from my daze.

Sucking in a deep breath, I answer, "I don't know where he was...I mean, I know. But I don't *really* know." I spoke my truth.

I'm sure he said he was working, but was he really? It wouldn't be the first time he came home smelling of sex and perfume. "Why don't you ask him where he was?"

"His attorneys are advising him to not answer some of our questions. Now tell me about this trespasser from the other night you mentioned," Detective Cruz says.

"Excuse me," Detective Valletta murmurs, stepping away to take a phone call, his husky voice answering exquisitely in Italian. His broad shoulders dwarfing my sizable front doorway.

I explain that I'm unsure who the trespasser was but describe everything I saw. "Should I have an attorney present right now?" I ask.

Her spine stiffens as she answers, "That's entirely up to you, but you're not being charged. Did you know the recent victim was an employee of your husband's?"

"Yes." I quickly add, "I saw it on television."

"He is romantically linked to each woman. In both cases, we believe he was the last known person to be seen with them."

She begins to scoot closer to me but stops, visibly questioning her position. Her scent becomes stronger and slides over me, offering smooth comfort like an old blanket.

"Do you know Brooke Sadler, his employee, had a lawsuit against your husband and his company that he settled out of court?"

I swallow hard as I shake my head. My eyes swell with tears that quickly blur my vision when she displays a picture on her cellphone of Brooke Sadler. In the photo, Brooke holds her silky chestnut hair back with her right hand to showcase fingerprint shaped bruises on the right side of her neck. The dark bruises disturbingly obvious on her fair skin. Detective Cruz slides to the next picture showing an inflamed lip and dried blood around the corner of her mouth.

"She claims Robert did this to her in his office three years ago." Detective Cruz slides to another picture of Brooke's arms that show more bruises shaped like large fingerprints.

I allow my face to fall into my hands.

"Brooke didn't tell anyone. She was very close with her family, but they didn't know about the lawsuit. Her attorney thinks she was embarrassed, but the attorney claims she felt obligated to move on with litigation after their relationship ended with physical abuse."

"Relationship..." The word escapes from my mouth. This is the first time I've ever considered his sexual activity outside of our marriage to be anything more than sex. My mind floods with the idea of what their relationship might have involved. Did they talk about their days with each other? Did he take her to dinner? Did he buy her gifts? Did he tell her he loved her? My shoulders slump further down with the weight of the word "relationship" resting on them.

"There's more, Sophia," she says, obviously feeling guilty for adding more to my fragile state.

I draw in a deep breath that raises my shoulders. Pushing my shoulders back, I give myself the strength to raise my head. My wet face rises to meet hers and our eyes meet. Her pity engulfs me.

"I'm sorry..." She shakes her head but forces more words from her mouth. "The first victim, Megan Coldwell, her husband has provided proof that Robert was with her the night she was murdered. And that their affair had been going on for about six months before her sudden death."

Her words heave into my stomach like a fist, forcing me to bend and clutch my knees with my sweaty palms. I'm being tortured by words, a feeling worse than any physical abuse.

She leans closer. "Here," she whispers, handing me her card. "You call me anytime, I mean anytime, and I'll be here within ten minutes."

With my head still spinning from the punch of her words, I reach for her card, using all my strength to do something so simple. Her delicate brown hand grazes mine and we both momentarily freeze in place, leaving our hands touching. I slowly move my index finger along the top of hers, feeling her soft skin slip under my own. Our gazes lock on our touching skin.

My head stops spinning, the pain from her words vanishes like mist clearing in the warm sun, and the room becomes deafeningly still.

My tears stop, and my vulnerability turns into something else. I'm infatuated with this woman and I can feel it in return. She looks again at my lips wet with tears, then gradually raises her eyes from my lips to my nose, then to my eyes. Her dark eyes turn a reddish-mahogany from the sunlight illuminating them.

The front door swings open and she jerks her hand from our exchange. We shift our eyes to Detective Valletta, who has his head down, looking at the phone in his hefty hand as he enters the room.

"We have to go." His deep voice is soft yet forceful. He stands at the opening to the room, not acknowledging me, watching Detective Cruz.

She stands abruptly. "Well, you have my card. We will be in touch." Her use of "we" removes any unspoken intimacy, inserting her unfriendly partner between us. I watch her as she takes one hurried step, then stops just as abruptly as she stood. Detective Cruz stares at her partner with an open mouth as if she's about to speak to him. Then she turns suddenly to meet my gaze. With a stiff spine and an authoritative tone, she says, "Sophia, we believe he's dangerous. Please…be careful."

I nod as I stand, offering a slight smile as I look over at Valletta, who is peering at Cruz. "I'll see you out," I offer with newfound calmness. I walk them to the front door, my stilettos clacking along the floor, echoing in our silence. I stand in my doorway, watching them march together to their car. Detective Valletta cocks his head towards Cruz, glancing down at her walking by his side. A look of worry splashes across his masculine face before they break their matching stroll to enter the car from opposite sides.

I step back into my house, relishing the desire flowing through my limbs.

After locking my door, I lean my back against it, resting my head back as a smile forces my cheeks to plump under my eyes. My hand reaches for my stomach to calm the butterflies, while the other rests fingertips on my smiling lips. The clarity of this strange control is a high I've been desperately searching for. A high that numbs the pain.

5

Old Impulses

Rebecca's infectious, chesty laugh hoots from across the brown paper-covered table in the corner of the restaurant, continuing her story as her cheeks blush from the wine. Her personality had fit me like a lost puzzle piece, then, without warning, she was a good friend reciting some comical story of something she's done or seen.

With the last sip of my vodka cranberry, I taste mostly vodka and try not to pucker my lips. "Let me get you another," Melanie squeaks as soon as the ice clinks on the bottom of my glass.

"No, I shouldn't. I have an early day tomorrow."

"Are you helping Rob with all this fuss I hear about Anexa?" Rebecca asks, referring to Anexa going international while lowering her gaze to receive the gossip.

I shake my head, offering a sheepish smile as the waiter

returns with my credit card, saving me from offering Rebecca a full answer. Melanie squints her green eyes at me, knowing full-well I dodged Rebecca's question on purpose.

A woman waves at our table as she walks towards the front door of the restaurant to leave. I don't recognize her, but I smile as Rebecca waves back.

"You know Katherine?" Melanie asks Rebecca with noticeable judgment.

"She knows my niece." Rebecca flicks her wrist, dismissing Melanie's judgment. "Did you see her Valentino Rockstud Leather T-Straps?" Rebecca asks, twisting her mouth.

"And in red," Melanie adds with her upper lip lifted in revulsion.

"They've always said that you can't buy class." Rebecca lifts her brows and purses her lips.

I hear the women, but don't partake in the conversation as I glance out the window, noticing it has stopped raining but the wind continues to whip red and brown leaves around the wet parking lot, reminding me of the wind on the rooftop in my dream that whips my hair and nightgown.

Melanie's voice lowers as she leans over the tabletop enough for her large breasts to rest on it. "Are these murders creepy or what?"

My spine stiffens as Rebecca answers obnoxiously loud. "Yes! Jesus! And they still haven't figured it out? I mean, what the hell is going on? I know the protesting is stifling resources, but come on!"

Melanie points her gaze at me. "How is Rob doing with… oh, what was her name? You know, the employee?"

"Her name was Brooke Sadler." I don't answer the part about Rob.

"Things are getting creepy around here, ya know? Like, I'm making sure my windows and doors are locked at night," Rebecca says. She lives alone, having been married once to a prominent attorney for a year. Yet, when she talks about marriage, she channels a war vet. A feeling I'm starting to understand.

Rebecca and Melanie continue to talk about the murders and the civil unrest. Both splash their fears across the table, trailing with echoes of ego, because who wouldn't want them as their victim? The richest women in the city, aside from myself, of course. My mind glazes over as I watch the wind dance with the leaves.

"I mean, the person committing the murders probably wants to get caught and go to jail, right? You know, for the fame," Rebecca screeches as she brings her glass to her lips, muting her assault on my ears momentarily.

I skate my gaze from the wet parking lot to Rebecca. "It's prison, not jail," I say, correcting her.

"What?" Rebecca asks drunkenly, gliding her moist glass across the paper-covered table.

"Never mind. It's just that, well, jail isn't for...prison is where murderers go."

Rebecca's bracelets jangle and jingle together as she waves her arms wildly in the air. "Well then, look at the expert we have right here." She flicks her eyes at Melanie, then back at me. She then pretends she has a microphone in her hand. Leaning across the table, pointing her imaginary microphone at me, she shrieks, "Sophia Claire! I understand your husband was the employer of one of the slain women. Do you have anything to say about that?"

Keeping my head down, I raise my eyebrows aggressively at her. "Rebecca, it's not funny. You can't make light of this. This," I point to her invisible microphone, "is not funny either."

Rebecca slides back into her place, the leather booth sounding off at her movement. Adjusting her top, she says, "Shit, Soph. I'm sorry. I guess I'm trying to make it less scary, ya know? The world seems to have gone crazy."

I offer a half smile and glance at Melanie, who has her face in her phone, pretending not to notice the tension that is slowly evaporating from our table. I glance around the almost empty restaurant as I politely state it's time to call it a night.

I know the world realizes who Brooke's employer was, but the callousness of Rebecca's question stings. Do others look at Rob and wonder if he has anything to say about Brooke? The thought sends me spiraling back down the void of Detective Cruz's words. What she told me about Rob's affairs with the murdered women and the embarrassment of the affairs scrapes at my ego. The bright lights of the world shining on my marriage is dizzying.

As we gather our belongings, the vibration of my cellphone spreads through my Saint Laurent handbag.

"Oh, ladies. I'm going to hang back," I say, waving my phone with Rob's photo lit brightly on the display. As they gesture their goodbyes, blowing kisses with open palms, I think about what excuse Rob will provide tonight.

Sitting back down in the bouncy leather booth alone, I twirl the ice melting in my glass as I listen to Rob say he'll be home late. He sweetly tells me not to wait up but offers no explanation.

"This is for you, from the gentleman in the suit at the bar," the waiter says as he slides another vodka cranberry onto my table.

I drop my phone into my handbag, fiddling with the gold chain on the strap as I lean around the waiter. I see a handsome man in a tailored black suit. He rises to his feet, then begins walking towards me. His black leather shoes gleam in the soft artificial light with each step of his long stride. His face—unshaved for two, maybe three days—doesn't smile, but instead offers an overconfident wink.

"May I sit?" he asks upon reaching my booth. His deep green eyes crinkle with a hint of a smile.

"I really rather you didn't."

He ignores my request, dipping into the booth across the table. My large paper-covered table grows incredibly small.

"Hi." He offers a cocky half smile and runs a hand through his thick coffee-colored hair. "A beauty such as yourself shouldn't eat alone."

"My friends just left. Which I'd bet you saw from the bar," I challenge him, tilting my head to the side.

A corner of his mouth curves up in a way that triggers a carnal desire in me. "Well, you've caught me," he says, raising his large palms to face me. "I did see you enjoying your dinner with two lady friends."

Uncomfortable silence creates thick air, prompting my throat to tighten.

"I really must be going," I say as I rise hastily.

"Please." He reaches for my arm, gripping it tight enough to stop me, but gentle enough to allow me to break free if I desired.

"Ben, I really should go," I protest.

"Sophia, I miss you. Please. Just sit and talk, that's all." He releases my arm. His large green eyes and crumpled brow beg for me to stay.

I appease him.

Benjamin Booth had almost always gotten his way with me. His smugness is subtly conveyed through intelligence, but his charm is undeniable. I always believed him to be the type of man who knew what he wanted and wasn't afraid to do what it took to get it.

Our affair provided me the attention of a man who only saw me in the room. A man who only craved my flesh—which is something Rob can't deliver.

Benjamin Booth was an excellent lover. I fit him perfectly.

I had ended it mostly because the guilt of an affair was overwhelming, even though I knew Rob continued his affairs. My marriage vows in the presence of God meant a great deal to me. I lost faith momentarily but was reminded to honor my husband and our vows through faith. Ben became erratic and possessive after I dismissed him from my life. He later lost his job as the director of policy for Trimble Laboratories because of his growing aggressive behavior.

He was the only affair I've allowed. When I met Ben at Anexa, he thrilled me. He quickly became my replica of happiness. My distraction. I hadn't realized how unhappy I was until I met Ben.

"How are you? You look beautiful." He reaches across the table for my hand. I glance down at his large, hot hand resting on mine, allowing memories of how I used to ache for him to wash over me in an intense wave.

"Ben, stop." I pull my hand from under his and reach for my mother's cross. My eyes pored over his face, again noticing how similar his features are to Rob's. He could easily be mistaken for him. "Was that you the other night? At my house?"

He ignores my question and speaks softly across the table. "I know you miss me. I know you…every inch."

Anxiety rattles through me, causing me to stand abruptly, hustling for the exit. My legs carry the deadweight that is my torso.

Ben promptly follows, attempting to stop me as he did before, but I jerk my arm out of his grasp, maintaining a steady pace for my car.

The large parking lot is almost barren with only a few cars. I see Ben's silver Audi parked next to my car; both are tucked away where the parking lot lights neglect to shine. The wind whirls my hair around my face and threatens to lift my skirt as my heels clack loudly on the wet asphalt.

"Sophia!" His voice is frenzied as he catches up to me, pinning me to my wet driver's side door.

"What?" I hiss through clenched teeth.

"I know you miss me. I know you think about me." He attempts to kiss me, but I quickly turn my head. But that doesn't stop his advances. He leans his body into mine, holding me firm against my car, as he slides his hand down my arm, the pressure extending it against my will.

"I miss your touch, Soph," he says, keeping his body firmly pressed against mine to hold me in place. "I miss you caressing the bulge in my pants in public while your voice whispers what you want from me. Your hot breath whispering things," Ben exhales as his eyes close tightly thinking about our memories together, "things you know will make me want you, pushing me to where I can't stand it any longer and have to have you."

"Get off me!" I writhe under the pressure of his body against mine. My skirt being tugged up by the wiggling against his body. "Ben!"

He presses his forehead against mine. "Your second favorite spot to be touched is right here," he cruelly whispers into my ear while circling his fingertip on the inside of my wrist. His hot breath warming my cold ear.

"The first, though, that's here," he says, shoving his hand up my skirt and forcefully kisses my mouth, smashing my lips into my teeth. "I think about you all the time, Soph. I think about how you love it when I pin you against a wall and shove my hand up your skirt, finding no panties in my way and feeling how wet you are from thinking about me. I miss finger fucking you until you're begging for me."

His jagged breath devours my ear as he forces his hand into my panties. "I miss you, Soph. I miss the way you smell. Your voice. The way you taste." He bites my earlobe as he removes his finger from inside me, then slides it into his mouth to taste me.

The need for power burns my belly as I wiggle out from his control. I heave my knee into his groin. "Fuck you!" I bark as he stoops over, moaning in agony. Scurrying into my car, I lock the doors and seriously consider backing over him as I reverse from the parking space.

Pulling out of the parking lot, I see Ben fall into his opened driver's side door through my rearview mirror. My anger turns into shame, then slides into remorse for having dismissed Ben so cruelly in the past. Benjamin Booth: the man who loved me more than any man ever did. His love for me consumed him, growing uncontrollable as he grew irresponsible.

His actions were always pointed at me with a devotion that showed through his behavior. His days without me were spent thinking about and craving me. The days with me he used to show how much I meant to him. His sacred high achieved from making me smile, laugh, and moan.

His actions tonight show how irrational his desire for me has become. He truly believes he needs me. After Rob fired him, he spiraled further into believing I was the answer to his happiness, as if having me would fix it all. I don't believe it to be true, but I don't doubt his belief. When a man loves a woman, she can become his ultimate weakness.

Arriving home, I find an empty house lit brightly, signaling Rob had come home before going back to work. I set my handbag down on my vanity in our bathroom, carefully slouching the chain strap down on the vanity, then slide my heels off, placing each in their designated area in our closet. After undressing, I step into the cold shower, gripping the bright chrome handle, turning it all the way to the right. Hot water bursts through the showerhead on the ceiling and stings my skin cooled by the autumn air.

Allowing the hot water to burn away the tension. The water slides down my body, triggering bumps to raise from my skin.

I tilt my head back and close my eyes, allowing the hot water to drench my hair.

As I stand under the cascade of hot water, my mind agonizes over Ben and his behavior tonight. Not so much his aggressiveness, but his increasing erraticism and the potential to tell Rob about our affair.

I wonder how Rob does it? How he keeps his affairs under control and quiet?

It's a talent.

6

Becoming Mrs. Claire

The first time we met, Rob shook my hand and said my name twice out loud. He said my name in a way where we both knew he would know my body and soul well. There was an instant glimmer of obviousness for us. I knew I could make him happy, and I knew he could make me happy. When he shook my hand and smiled his gorgeous smile, I felt it. He was dating someone at the time, and so was I. None of that mattered, though. When we touched, we knew. When we explored each other's faces, we knew. When we made love, we knew.

We met on a clear night in downtown Seattle while at the Fairmont Olympic Hotel for a fundraiser benefitting the Seattle Children's Hospital. The room dense with adults in expensive and impressive Halloween costumes dancing to classic Halloween music. I was standing next to my then boyfriend, who was dressed badly as Waldo in a red-and-white-striped long-sleeved shirt, red-and-white-striped beanie with a white ball on top, and embarrassingly tight denim pants. We stood together scrutinizing an item up for auction as my Catwoman costume suffocated me. I regretted wearing my hair half down because I was overheating in my tight pleather bodysuit. He left to fetch himself a drink without asking if I wanted one. I watched him walk away in his ridiculous costume, and that's when I first saw Rob. He was dressed as a Viking. His soft gaze slammed in my direction, hitting me like a large wave from across the dance floor.

We walked on opposites sides around the ocean of dancing bodies, floating to each other in what felt like moments. When we were face-to-face, we didn't speak. Instead, we observed each other, standing in slowed time together. I studied his handsome face half hidden under a dark beard. One side of his face lightly kissed by the city lights descending from the towering windows of the ballroom, the other strobing with light from the dance floor.

We spoke through our eyes, reading each twinkle. Cheesy, yes. But it was the most intense, unexplainable moment of my life. I've never been drawn to someone with such magnetism. Nothing else in the room mattered. I cracked a smile first, and he followed. He extended his hand, and with his exquisite accent said his name.

I now understand why people say *when you know, you know*.

Over the next week, he sent me a bouquet of four dozen roses each workday to my office. Each day was a different color, but the arrangement was identical with only strongly scented, flawless roses with no filler flowers. They were the most beautiful arrangements and my office smelled like a perfect summer day. It seemed everyone in my office knew who he was, except for me. The women were buzzing with excitement each time a new arrangement arrived from the CEO of Anexa, begging me to read the attached card aloud.

Monday, he sent red roses and the card read, "When can I see you again?"

Tuesday, he sent pink roses and the card simply read, "Dinner this Friday?"

Wednesday, he sent white roses and the card simply read, "Another day wasted."

Thursday, he sent apricot roses and the card read, "I can't stop thinking about you."

Friday, he sent purple roses with no card.

In place of the usual card, there was a typed letter in a sealed envelope with only his initials watermarked on the front.

I closed my office door, shooing everyone away to read it alone. I tore open the envelope with enthusiasm and held the single piece of paper in front of me. I was so excited to get a letter from him. Who writes letters anymore?

The letterhead had his initials in a bold yet modern font and his greeting to me was "Ms. Sophia Case."

In the letter, he described it as "time itself had slowed just for us," confirming he felt what I did. He continued by describing an irresistible feeling to know me and said he would leave me alone, but I will always be the one he wonders about. He ended the letter by offering a date and time: he would be at the Deep River airport waiting for me, and if I did not show, he wouldn't pursue me further.

The significant thrill I felt when near him was reinforced each day he sent flowers. Each day I woke up thinking of him. Each day I eagerly awaited my newest flower arrangement. The butterflies that danced in my belly, forcing a smile onto my lips, reinforced my desire to meet him at the airport.

When we met at the airport for our first official date, he was freshly shaved, allowing me to see the facial features that were hidden behind the Viking beard he grew for Halloween. He was even more handsome than when we first met. His dark hair long enough to grab a fist full and eyes an intense light brown.

He flew us to Seattle in a friend's tiny plane. I had always been a nervous flyer, but with him I felt daring. I trusted his power. He affected me in such a way that I felt impulsive but stable, fearless but on edge, in control but influenced. In Seattle, we did the touristy stuff like visit the Sky View Observatory at the top of the Columbia Center building and the Chihuly Garden.

After dinner, he ushered me to the top of the Hilton where he explained there had once been a restaurant but is now empty space. The view was remarkable. We stood close to one another, overlooking the dark Puget Sound with its lighted boats floating past each other on the calm black water. The lights of the city streets below and surrounding buildings illuminated our faces.

That's where we kissed for the first time. He pressed me against the window, lifting my chin to meet his height, then kissed me softly. As his kiss grew deeper, he began controlling my tongue with his as he reached down, gripping my hips to pull me tightly against him. When he broke from my lips, my self-control somehow succeeded in not begging for more. His wet kiss was better than most lovers I've had. He immediately became my addiction.

After a few months, we were dating exclusively. Looking back, I understand now that his power I felt wasn't power at all, but instead manipulation. The way he worded his expressions, the tone he used, his body language. He managed everyone around him in this way. It's quite a thing to watch—that is, when it isn't being directed at you.

Soon, I began to see the cracks in his foundation of control. When he didn't have it, his skin crawled. When he couldn't obtain it, he would become angry, enraged even. However, no one can control all people and situations. Not even Robert Charles Claire.

One evening, before moving in together, we agreed to dinner at Anthony's on the Columbia River, a pleasant seafood restaurant with an excellent view. I sat at our table while Rob went to the restroom to wash after a long workday. While I was admiring the moonlight dancing on the Columbia River, the server arrived and began cheerfully spouting the specials of the evening. She was pretty, with thick, shimmering natural blonde hair, a symmetrical face, and an athletic frame. As she was taking the drink order, Rob arrived at the table. When their eyes met, she froze. Her mouth left open mid-sentence and her eyes widened. Rob, though, only froze for a moment, then casually continued to glide his long, well-dressed body effortlessly into his seat across from me. She reached for her poise, confirmed the drinks, then hurried away.

"What was that?" I asked, completely confused about what had just happened.

"What?"

I leaned over the table, admiring his face lit by a single candle placed in between us, and whispered, "With the server. Do you know her?"

"Maybe she fancies me," he answered teasingly, offering a sly smile.

While Rob moved intently between his phone and the menu, I glanced across the room and saw the server sobbing while a male server consoled her. Another server worked our table for the evening and I never saw her again.

That night he made love to me roughly and forcefully. It wasn't unkind, just different. Each thrust long and full of aggression.

As our life continued together, he introduced me to people from his life. The men always kind and gentlemanly, and the wives always relieved he was settling down, or maybe they were just happy he would stop tempting their husbands by parading his latest perky fling around. I made friends quickly with many of the wives, and from them was introduced to various social circles. However, some women I met fired looks at me—glares I couldn't quite decipher—and would avoid me. The looks bordered on pity or jealousy, possibly a mixture of both.

He was a lady's man. I've heard stories. I didn't care, though, because he was soon to be my husband. My past didn't count, and neither did his. I should have seen the warning signs, but I was just too blinded by bliss and ignored them all. Even the events I saw with my own eyes, like the one at his office with Brooke Sadler three years ago.

I had visited him unannounced. We were newly married and

still so madly in love. We had just moved into our new home, and I was positively elated. I was planning our home decor, our children's first few years, and my future as Mrs. Claire. We had also decided it was best that I quit my job; I was going to be a full-time mommy to a handful of children, after all.

Arriving at his office, I found him sitting at his desk, studying paperwork in the dim light only a lamp could provide. He always appeared so handsome when deep in thought. I watched him lovingly for a moment. My eyes taking in his tousled dark hair and his strong, thick neck, until I heard a woman's voice from the corner of his office hidden from my view. That little voice we all have deep inside hissed at me to hide, so I quickly tucked behind the wall and listened to the woman's voice as my stomach quivered and hands shook.

"I don't understand," she pleaded through tears.

He continued to read his paperwork, ignoring her. He ran his fingers through his hair, as if brushing off her urgency.

"Rob!" She raised her weeping voice to catch his attention.

"Look! I don't have time for this, Brooke. Come off it."

"You're a smug bastard. I fucking hate you!" she yelped through sobs.

Rob hurled his paperwork into the air, and I ducked further behind the wall, his quick movement frightening me. She whimpered as he whispered sharp words, using a short, aggressive tone.

I distinctly heard her weeping voice confirm his words back to him. "You'll fucking end me?"

I needed to see. I had to see. I risked it and peeked.

He was holding her against the wall with his hand tightly

wrapped around her petite throat. His face so close to hers that he could kiss her. The tendons in his neck tightened into thick cords bulging next to pulsing veins, and his lips tightened around his white teeth like a predator ready to strike. Brooke's soft face was shackled with fear and her cheeks wet from tears.

The paperwork he had been studying intently scattered messily on the floor.

I had never seen Rob angry, let alone violent.

I scurried away. I ignored it. I didn't want to know. I told myself she was an old flame he had extinguished since our marriage and she wasn't taking it well.

He came home that night with scratch marks on his neck. I ignored those, too.

By then, I was beginning to see his darkness hiding deep below his perfected surface. He hides it so well. He can be such a charming, witty, and disarming man. However, there is something inside him that can slowly crawl over his goodness, dimming his light.

Something vicious.

He has directed this side of him at me only once. I had given my sister, Cassidy, two thousand dollars to start an Etsy shop of her creations. I knew it wasn't going to be fruitful, as Cassidy always gives up on things once they become mildly difficult, but I love that she tries. After all, two thousand dollars to my husband is one suit in a closet full of suits.

He had come home aggravated. Worried, I asked what was wrong. With his strong shoulders up to his ears and his brown eyes squinting, he asked me about the money I had given Cassidy. I explained that I didn't think anything of it, as if it wasn't a big deal because I didn't think that it was. The muscles in his chest flexed under his shirt, and his teeth gritted with an angry growl before he gripped a crystal vase we received as a wedding present from my godmother and hurled it, smashing it against the wall behind me. I had bruises on my arms from where he gripped so tightly as he spat through clenched teeth that I was to ask the next time.

To any other woman, he may have been intimidating, and they may have been frightened by his behavior. I only saw a pathetic man who had lost control momentarily and was throwing a childish fit. I didn't believe he could actually hurt me.

7

The Watchman

I dream again that I am wearing the white cotton nightgown, its thickness covering my arms and hanging off my shoulders down to my ankles. I walk barefoot through the night's sky with city lights glowing beneath me. A breeze that I cannot feel—neither warm nor cold—pressed the nightgown against my body as I grasp my mother's cross that hangs from my neck.

Meeting the edge of the roof, the breeze now a light wind whipping my long brown hair around my face and nightgown-covered shoulders. Stepping to the edge, my toes curl on the ledge, and I glance down at the unfamiliar city street below. The wickedness radiates from the person behind me, just as their sin is unmistakably familiar.

I rotate my head, careful not to test my balance in an attempt to meet the eyes of the wicked one behind me. I find Rob standing behind me, alone. His body in its regular professional attire but his head is that of a demon with a serpent tongue split up the middle. The skin of his gelatinous face a mangy bright red, oozing from pus-filled sores. His mouth bends with strong words as veins protrude from his neck from the frenzied effort, though his exertion in yelling through the wind fails; his voice cannot penetrate the now deafening wind atop the tall city building.

He steps closer, his lips bending in a familiar way; he is saying my name. His serpent tongue curls each time he speaks it, concentrating on the S in Sophia. He stands directly behind me, the wind whipping his tie in his face as he reaches for me with alarm twisting his brow, fear detonating in his brown eyes. And then I wake up. And like the times before, I feel comfort in the dream. As if all life's uncertainties have molded into an obvious simplicity that leave me feeling free.

The new sunlight creates a bluish light that beams through the windows of our bedroom. I stretch, then wiggle out of our massive bed, slip on my silk robe, and step slowly and quietly out the bedroom door. I half close it, hoping Rob won't be woken by my activity.

I lower myself gently onto the oversized cushioned chair in the sitting room with my closed laptop on my lap. I wait, listening for movement from the bedroom before I open the device. The artificial light burns my eyes. I squint, waiting for them to grow used to the bright display illuminating my face in our still mostly dark living room.

Rob had laid asleep in our bed while I lay awake beside him. My mind wandering through the dark alleys of worry until my phone vibrated with an alert that made it impossible to stay in bed.

Leaving a tab open on Facebook, I sit facing the entryway Rob might use, allowing me to click on the tab for Facebook and away from the tab I'm reading in case he was to walk in. A move Rob must use daily.

I click on Google and search for the article I was alerted to—a new murder of a third woman. I begin clicking on each new article I haven't read before. By now, even big-time newspapers have taken this story and made it national.

The local news published the recent murder first, describing it as different than the others because of how the woman was found. Instead of in her home, she was found by construction workers in a brand-new housing development that had just begun dirt work for new homes. The neighborhood sits high on a treeless hillside, with nothing but freshly laid asphalt roads, compacted dirt, and boundary sticks showing where each new house will be built.

One article displays a single picture of the scene: the woman's oversized shiny black SUV parked sideways in the middle of one of the neighborhood's new asphalt roads, with its driver's side door wide open.

The article shows a flattering picture of Rosey Franklin, the recent murder victim. The photo displays her and a friend at what appears to be a concert; a picture I didn't see on her Facebook. Her thick black hair hangs past her shoulders and cascades down to her tiny waist. Her plump lips stained red with perfectly placed lipstick, and her chocolate eyes flirt with a hint of a smile, just as she did in the photo of her in Atlanta.

The article explains she was driving home but ended up a

few blocks from her house—in the new development—where she stopped her car as the sun set, stepping out of her car to get help, but fell unconscious in just a few steps. Once the sun rose the next day, she was found by workers of the new development—car still running, music still playing.

She's lucky the coyotes didn't get to her first. Her music must have kept them away.

The police mention a Starbucks cup with what they believe to be tea that will be tested for fentanyl. The article ends by asking if anyone had seen Rosey the day of her death.

I consider the drug again and its delivery method, then the schedule which it adheres to. It only takes moments to work, which means she must have taken the first sip of her drink as she entered her neighborhood, becoming confused and growing increasingly fatigued as she drove through the steep hills and sharp turns of the High Lakes housing community.

The unexpected euphoria I feel when studying these murders turns into alarm when I hear Rob clear his throat as it echoes from the bedroom.

My stomach drops as the unwelcome memory of Detective Cruz warning me to be careful sneaks into my mind. I look down at my fingers resting on the laptop, allowing the brief shock of the memory to pass. My fingers begin to tremble. The ominous silence of the room is only interrupted by the thought that Cruz may be right. Do I need to be careful?

Sitting motionless, every noise magnified, I wait to hear him pad down the hallway, but no further noise is made.

I click on another article that discusses a vigil that was held for the women last night in Deep River's public park. The park only illuminated by the candles people held. Attendees came together to pray for the slain women and show their support for the investigation. The video link directs me to a video of a crowded stage filled with family members of the murdered women, police officers, and advocates. Each family had a moment in the spotlight. Some used it to showcase who the loved one was. However, one used their moment on stage to blame. This was Brooke Sadler's father. His white mustache bounced as his lips pursed with each condemning word. He ended his anger-filled moment in the spotlight by stating Anexa mistreated Brooke and her superior's actions must be brought to light.

Why didn't he just say it? His daughter had a lawsuit settled out of court with my husband; a detail Detective Cruz shared with me. His attorney probably suggested he not mention specifics. It was a smart suggestion knowing my husband loves to exhaust people with the amount of money he can spend in court. He not only loves it; he gets off on it.

Detective Cruz stands in the corner of the stage, her small frame lost in a sea of dark blue police uniforms. Her light grey pant suit distinct against the dark blue, but her tiny stature melting into the muscular wall of men.

I return to Google and type *Detective Cruz Deep River*.

Various articles pop up, but only a few relating to the recent murders in Deep River. Many of the articles are of her mother— the famous and beautiful Leeza Lopez. I click on various articles about Leeza, showing her at glamorous Hollywood events for the films she was in. But the most recent articles explain her sad and slow death from bone cancer. One photograph shows her sitting in a chair, her skin hanging from her bones and her head adorned with a silk scarf. A little girl sits on her lap. The photo is captioned, "Leeza and Adella."

The articles claim Leeza died a millionaire, leaving her millions to her daughter, Adella Cruz. My nose scrunches with disbelief. Not only does Cruz do everything to avoid her looks given to her by her mother, but she chooses to continue a career in law enforcement. My skin tingles with surprise as my mind searches for the reason why someone who looks like her wouldn't want to live a different life, given her financial freedom.

After my initial surprise dissipates, I continue searching through articles that focus on Detective Adella Cruz. Sifting through various articles about her mother, I find a headline that catches my attention. It's five years old, but still relevant. Opening the link, a picture of young Cruz greets me, her spine stiff as she proudly stands in her naval uniform. The title of the article mentions her only as "Cadet Cruz," and goes into detail about her ambition to become a police detective after retiring from the Navy, a far cry from her mother's footsteps.

The meat of the article describes her older sister's death in Deep River as a suspicious overdose, unfolding the sad circumstances after she dated a man, Ricky Vasquez, who was well known for sex trafficking and drug manufacturing in California and Eastern Washington.

Cruz had been so wounded by her sister's death; her soul ached to fix the world. Which explains her instinctive need to help me. She was quoted as saying, "The Navy has been good to me. But I want to go home [to Deep River] to serve my people, which is why I've studied hard for my exams to become a detective for the DRPD."

I scroll up, looking at her tight smile in the photograph. Age has barely touched her and, if anything, she has only grown more beautiful.

I wiggle to the side of the oversized chair; the sun now reflecting awkwardly off my screen.

I continue searching for anything related to the murders—something that has become a morbid hobby of mine—and another article catches my eye. Brooke Sadler's beautiful, youthful face shines a bright smile. The newspaper states the police may have a lead, thanks to a tip.

The article reports that a man had been seen leaving both Brooke's condo as well as Megan Coldwell's house. The neighbors carefully detail the male's appearance and the details match. The article finishes with a warning to all women in the area between the ages of twenty and forty to be aware of their surroundings, keep in contact with loved ones throughout the day, and be cautious around strangers.

I can't count the times since these murders started that I've been told to be careful by friends, acquaintances, or even strangers. The city is anxiously awaiting another body or news of an arrest. My mind chews on the thought that Rob essentially paid off Brooke in an out-of-court settlement. It's not as if court actions are foreign to my husband or his businesses; it's the cost of doing business in the pharmaceutical management and research industry.

"Babe?" Rob's voice breaks through the deafening silence of the room, causing me to jump and my laptop to fall open to the floor. I instinctively grab my chest and exhale sharply before reaching for the laptop and darting my mouse to the Facebook tab.

"Jesus, Rob."

"Sorry," he chuckles, his voice still rough from sleep. "How long have you been up?"

"Oh, not long; I couldn't sleep."

He enters the sitting room, his naked muscular body fully illuminated by the bright new sun.

"What are you doing?" he asks, walking to me.

"Facebook," I answer. His eyes dart to my screen, then to my face.

"Anything worth sharing?" he asks, his eyes burrowing into mine. I shake my head. "Are you ready for today?" he asks as he grazes his hand down the back of my head. I nod. "We have to be there in a few hours," he says as he reaches for my laptop, setting it on the coffee table, then grips my hands to stand me up. "Come," he whispers with a smile on his lips as he pulls me to the bedroom to crawl back into bed with him.

We arrive at the stadium where Rob will be playing in a charity flag football game. While I know his actions are for a charity, it's hard not to see his pride glow with all the attention.

We meet Abe Brown at the entrance to the locker room. His tall, thin body already dressed to play. He tilts his hat with his team's name on it in an overly theatrical gesture. "Are the hats necessary?" he asks, his Scottish accent thick with sarcasm.

"Stop it. You look handsome," I assure him as he kisses my cheek in greeting.

"Alright, my love. I shall see you after. Let me hear you scream for me." Rob squeezes me, arching his neck to kiss me.

The coolness of the fall morning leaves behind a dew on the metal stands and I'm thankful I brought a cushion to sit on. I button my diamond quilted Burberry jacket as I sit in the stands alone, looking for a familiar face, wondering why they chose flag football for this event.

Rob enters the field in his uniform and baseball cap that signifies the team and charity he is playing for. He lifts it off his head and waves it at the crowd as the announcer goes through the roster. I hear women scream at his name and painfully notice I'm not one of them.

Unexpectedly, my thoughts float to Ben. Directly after our ending, he had fits of demanding I meet him. Demanding I see him "or else." His threats balanced on the sharp edge of telling Rob about us or harming himself.

I know ending our relationship was the right thing to do yet I still miss him and what we had, but not who he has become. I miss his laugh, kiss, and how loved I felt with him. The guilt of knowing I broke him settles on my chest until I notice a man with a shaved head walking up the concrete steps with his hands in his jean pockets, his eyes locked on me. He steps close enough that the greying stubble on his burly jaw shows.

He sits uncomfortably close to me. His proximity forcing me to look up at his face, which is already looking down at mine.

"Hi, Sophia. My name is Mark. You and I have people in common."

"Okay," I say slowly with confusion. "What can I do for

you?" I ask, searching for a normal connection to my world and this man.

"Sophia, I know your husband." His tone earnest as we both look out over the field. Rob, oblivious to the man as he and Abe point at each other from across the field and laugh at an inside joke.

"Great, what can I do for you?" I repeat.

"I know what your husband has done." I feel him look at me, but I don't dare turn my head back towards him to make eye contact.

Silence.

"Sophia," he presses, "he's dangerous. Men like him you don't see coming until it's too late." .

"What?" I glance at him just as he glances at the field again. I'm thankful his eyes don't meet mine, giving me a chance to study his sharp facial features and curved lips. His icy blue eyes glower at Rob.

"Abraham seems to be a good man. Busy man. Successful in his own right, unlike Robert, who comes from family money," he snarls.

He's right. Abe is an intelligent man. Abe made his own way in the world and it made him stronger, smarter, and bolder than someone like Rob who had it all given to him.

The sun breaks through the morning clouds and warms my skin. I become fiercely aware of my heart hammering against my ribs in the newly found heat.

Still looking at him, I say, "You sound like you've done your homework, Mr…" I leave empty air for him to insert his full name.

His chin tilts to the sun with a sharp nod at Rob, who is waving to someone on the opposite side of the stands. "Robert hasn't met his conquest for the evening yet." His voice mocks me. My lip curls and my breathing becomes heavier as anger warms my stomach.

His gaze still on Rob, he continues, "I know your husband is a philanderer, which you already know but pretend not to. I know you, too, Sophia. I know about Benjamin."

He stiffens as his open palms run up and down his jean-covered thighs, causing his muscular arms to flex with each thrust forward. "You know more women will die. It might be you, the beautiful *Sophia Claire*," his voice easily slides back to mocking me again. I notice a tattoo on the inside of his right wrist made up of a cluster of stars.

To anyone but me, this man would sound paranoid and crazy, but I recognize that he is telling the truth as it is laid out before him.

"Sophia, please. Do you know how he kills them?" I stay silent, allowing his voice to fill me, drying the saliva in my mouth. "He uses four times the amount of fentanyl needed to kill someone. He pours it into their drink after...after he has completed his *conquest*." He pauses with a harsh inhale. "I just don't understand how he chooses which ones to kill," he says, grasping for the answer as if it's right in front of him.

I glance at Rob, who is now standing rigidly upright, staring at me and the unknown man. My skin grows tight around my neck and my tongue seizes in my dry mouth.

"He's dangerous. Do you not understand? You are in danger." He's sounding more and more like a lunatic.

Turning my head as a soft breeze wafts hair around my face, I meet his panicked gaze before he notices Rob is now pointing at us. "He sees me," the man says as he rushes to his feet, then over his shoulder, he says, "He knows I'm watching him," before staggering away quickly, then ducking out of sight.

I glance at Rob again, with his head now back in the game, and I know that as delusional as the strange man sounds, he has some information correct, but my husband isn't a murderer.

8

Paradise

Rob had come home in a great mood after the game. He had gone out with Abe and some of the other players for drinks. I don't remember exactly what the root of his good mood was other than it had something to do with Anexa's growth.

I waited for Rob to ask who the strange man was sitting next to me in the stands, I even crafted the perfect lie, but he never asked. He also didn't say anything about the murdered women being his employee, friend, or lover, just as I didn't mention my recent encounters with the strange man, Ben, or the detectives.

Rob's music echoes from the bathroom down the long hallway where he showers, faintly stirring the still air in the kitchen. I begin rummaging through the pantry to find a snack to quench my low energy after our love making. I glide to the refrigerator, unsatisfied by the selection in our pantry, choosing a tomato to slice and sprinkle with salt. My mouth waters eagerly for the salty wetness.

Rob's music stops, allowing me to hear the rain hit our large windows that face east. I stare out the window above my kitchen sink as I wash the tomato and contentment washes over me. Autumn evenings filled with grey clouds put my soul at ease.

Rob strolls into the kitchen, freshly showered, wearing only a crisp white towel around his waist. His hair still wet and slicked back perfectly. The wetness making it appear jet black. He can be so charming and loving when he wants to be. It can be challenging to understand what is manipulation or what is the truth.

I slice delicately through the plump tomato as he slips behind me, slowly so I don't cut myself. His musky vanilla scent swirls through the air around me.

"Let's take a holiday." He wraps an arm around my waist.

I giggle, "A holiday?"

"We can go back to that place you liked so much in Maui. Remember that house?"

Yes, I remember that house. We visited it twice. Once before we were married and once a year into our marriage. It's owned by someone he does business with and is forty feet from the surf. We made love in every room of that house, twice. It is private and romantic. The sunsets, the sound of the waves crashing in our backyard, the eroticism of two people in love in paradise. It was heaven.

I'd asked to go back a few times, but he had always given the excuse of being too busy.

"The one in Kihei?" I ask, playing the fool.

"Yeah," he says as he whirls me around to face him.

"Wouldn't that be ace? Just the two of us." He kisses me softly and slowly, making my knees weak. "I asked and it's available." His voice lowers as he leans down, lightly pressing his nose to mine. "There is a flight available tomorrow morning and we'd come back Monday."

"Really?" I can't hide the excitement building in me as my cheeks plump under my eyes from a large smile.

"Yes! Let's do it." His British accent growing thicker with his excitement.

I throw my arms around his neck, balancing on my tippy toes to reach his lips. He bends at his waist, meeting my waiting lips as he wraps one arm around my waist, cupping my face with the other hand.

God, I love this man. He squeezes me in return, lifting my feet from the ground.

"I'll book the flights. You pack for us." His teeth peek from behind his lips, crooked from a grin, as he swivels on his heels.

I nod at his command and watch his tight ass flex with each step from under the white towel tied tightly around his waist.

His cellphone ringtone echoes into the kitchen. I hear his deep voice answer then the door to the bathroom close. I peer down the hallway to our bedroom, wondering if I could creep close enough without him noticing. Instead of letting suspicion dampen my joy, I turn around to my tomato sitting on the counter, ignoring the irritating feelings of jealousy and distrust.

Taking a single nibble from my sliced tomato, I throw the remainder into the garbage and collect our suitcases from the garage, as directed. I pack for my husband frequently. He is such a capable man, but Jesus, he needs taking care of in some respects.

After I pack for us both, tucking our full luggage near the door, we lay in bed and *really* talk for the first time in months. We don't make love, but instead share our delight over our trip tomorrow. Together, we gush about how crazy life has become for us both, and also how far we have come together and how proud we are of the life we created.

We arrive in Maui drunk in love, elated by each other's company. Someone on the plane had asked if we were on our honeymoon, and we both giggled.

The house is just as I remember it. Beautiful, extravagant, and ours for the next few days.

We unpack, quickly making the place our own. Rob gathers wine for us and we meet on the lavish back porch complete with an infinity pool that overlooks the beach. The property is situated perfectly, taking advantage of the trade winds that tender a refreshing tropical breeze.

He extends his hand, offering a glass of wine. "Cheers, my love."

Instead of reaching for it, I step away from him, and his eyebrows furrow in confusion. I remove my dress, letting it pool around my feet on the concrete patio, revealing my naked body. I slip into the pool and he follows with our wine.

We hover near the edge of the pool, sipping our wine, watching the turquoise waves dance on the white sand beach.

"This is really delicious wine," he murmurs. I can tell he's still a little tipsy from the booze on the plane.

"Yes. You know, it tastes like the one I voted for in my wine club. You remember?"

"Yes, I do." He kisses me.

"I think I still want to open the tasting room." We had argued intensely about me opening a tasting room before, but my words slip easily through the alcohol. I wanted it. He didn't.

I wait for his response.

"I think you have done very well with the speculative homes," he says, trying to fight through the booze to gain control over my assertiveness.

"I've done well with all my endeavors," I add.

"Yes. Why not! You should have what you desire. You deserve it." He sets his glass on the infinity edge and reaches for mine. Before he can grasp it, I gulp the last of the wine and offer a sinister smile. He embraces me in his strong arms, and I wrap my legs around him, locking my feet together tightly around his waist. We bob as one in the warm pool water.

He squeezes me tightly. My mother's cross props itself between us, stabbing us both.

"Ouch!" Rob rubs where the cross left an indentation on his chest.

"That's a first," I laugh, and clutch the necklace I haven't removed since my mother's death.

"I guess crosses really do work for protection," he teases, and kisses my lips.

I rub the mark it left on my chest as Rob grips the back of my neck. His large hand eclipsing my small neck, "I love you, Soph," his voice soft. I squeeze him harder with both my arms and legs.

"I love you more, Robbie."

"Robbie? Talk about nicking a moment!" He smiles large,

causing his magnetic brown eyes to squint tightly.

"What's wrong, *Robbie*?" I know he hates being called Robbie; it's what his mother calls him when she's about to say something provoking. The woman plays emotional chess for sport.

He squeezes me sharply and playfully. "YOU know what's wrong with Robbie." Then in a mocking tone of his mother, "Robbie, darling, haven't you got time to visit?"

We snicker together, twirling slowly as one with the water gently rushing around us.

"We actually should visit your mother soon. I do miss London, too," I admit, resting my chin on his wet shoulder after securing the cross flat to my chest.

He ignores the comment and changes direction. "Let's go to Little Beach."

"Not just yet," I say, reaching below the water to touch him.

"I'm up for it," he says gently over the sound of the wind whipping through the palm trees. His lips slowly cover his perfect teeth to kiss me, as his eyes flare with passion.

His love is like it once was. I sincerely feel it. I'm a woman who is truly loved by the man she loves, a feeling beyond any drug. Our sex had been like a drug to us both because we craved each other the way one would crave their next fix.

I'm beyond blissful. I do my best to ignore the irritating complications awaiting us back home.

I can fix it somehow.

We play in the surf all day, watching the naked people of all shapes and sizes on the nude beach. Rob keeps his shorts on and I go topless.

We eat mahi-mahi tacos from our favorite taco truck parked at the neighboring beach.

I love the way he walks proudly with me by his side. His attention here has warmed something inside me, but I know I can only hold his attention for so long.

His cellphone rings from inside his beach shorts. He quickly reaches into his pocket to silence it.

As we walk back to our car from Little Beach, I notice a pathway thick with overgrown vegetation. A single wooden post stands to the side of the overgrown path. Vines and bulky green leaves have camouflaged it, taking the wood back into nature. The post holds no sign, only an old carved marking displayed five feet high. As we step closer to the post, I notice it's the same symbol making up the small chrome pin I saw on Rob's desk the night of the trespasser. I break from Rob's hand, stepping close to the post that wields the symbol.

His phone rings again and he ignores my wandering off the path to retrieve it. He quickly silences the phone call again, shoving his cell back into his pocket.

"Does this look familiar to you?" I ask him as I trace the old carving with my index finger. Tracing one thick, continuous line that creates the pyramid shape, continuing onto the line that creates an infinity symbol running vertical through the pyramid.

He stays on the main pathway, his toes digging into the sand nervously as he downturns his lips and shakes his head.

"Hmmm. It does to me, and I can't place it," I lie, then step back to the path, reaching for his hand that's extended and waiting for mine. I look up to him and ask one more time, "Are you sure?"

"Yes, Soph," he chuckles. "I've never seen it before." He releases my hand and stretches his arm around me, gripping my shoulders, pulling me under his arm and into his side as we sway together.

When we arrive back to the house, there's a surprise candlelit dinner waiting for me on our patio with hypnotic Hawaiian music. The house's staff brings us various foods and drinks Rob had arranged. Rob even requested Kulolo to be served, my favorite Hawaiian dessert. We laugh, drink, and eat as his lies and cheating, the man from the tag football game, the detectives, and my bizarre encounter with Ben attempt to eclipse my happiness.

While I'm sure Rob doesn't know about Ben, paranoia haunts me at times because of Rob's behavior the week he fired Ben. I was always so careful, planning my time with Ben meticulously. If Rob knew, he would have made me pay for it for sure.

Together in a cushioned cabana bed overlooking the ocean, we watch the moonlight dance rhythmically on the ocean. I rest my back on his chest, reaching above my head to play with his thick dark hair.

"My love?" His voice glides smoothly over the sound of the waves crashing.

"Yes?"

"The woman…one of the women who was murdered… Brooke Sadler, she was an employee of mine."

Still twisting his hair in my fingers, I gaze out at the Pacific Ocean. "I know," I say as trepidation swirls in my stomach.

9

Friendly Stranger

Benjamin Booth's crisp tailored suit blended perfectly within the sea of suits around us. He had looked at me when we were introduced like he knew me. I had heard his name before, as I'm sure he'd heard mine, but his green eyes squinted at me, as if trying to place me in his catalogue of blissful memories. I also gazed a little too long, attempting to make sense of the familiarity. After shaking hands, we left them joined in place in the space between us. Ben's eyes narrowed, his gaze burrowing into mine. Their green varying in shades, starting with a deep green circling the iris that fades into a light brown around his pupil.

The woman introducing us tried her best to ignore the exchange between us. She awkwardly cleared her throat, popped up onto her toes before saying something about the time, and rushed me away to another hurried introduction.

Each introduction was bumpy with shaky words once she told the other person I was the wife of Robert Charles Claire—the founder of Anexa.

But Ben's words were not shaky; instead, they were confident and considerate. He felt like an old friend, with layers of complexity. My heart was at ease with him immediately, and his softness towards me was flattering.

We first met when the company he worked for had visited Anexa's headquarters in Deep River for a private tour of the new campus. Several companies visited Anexa over a week's time, from those who sold and stored gelatin capsules, to the laboratories who manufactured for Anexa. Everyone glowed with excitement to see where their company's office was located on the campus, taking in the new state-of-the-art facility. While I had seen the impressive new campus, and had even watched it be built, I was curious what the company tours involved, so I decided to join one at the last minute after having lunch with Rob.

Ben's company was Trimble Laboratories, a manufacturer of various synthetic opioid pain medication for Anexa. As the director of policy, Ben oversaw policy research and communicated with stakeholders, the public, the media, and Robert Claire. Like me, though, Ben was just a chess piece in the game of life for Rob. A severable appendage that could be replaced if need be.

I strolled near Ben during our groups' campus tour, looking away each time our eyes met. At that moment, I was thankful to be in a group of people I didn't know. Each face that saw mine didn't offer that familiar slight smile that told me they knew who I was; that cordial half smile that said, *I'm on my best behavior because I know who you are.*

An impatient longing in me begged to know about Ben Booth: where he was from, who he's loved, and why he kept smiling at me through the crowd like I'd told a terrible joke and he was taking pity on me. His smile was subtle, barely visible on his taut lips that curved upwards on one side. His crinkled eyes were what gave away his amusement. Each time his smiling deep green eyes met with mine, my stomach sank a little as if riding a roller coaster that jerked into its first intense plunge.

The familiarity was puzzling, yet strangely comforting. His appearance so much like Rob's, but that wasn't the root of my attraction to him. In him, I had found an old friend whom I had never met before.

Dennis, the escort for our tour group, was a gruff old man whose voice was deep and broken from decades of cigarette smoke. A tour group member had asked a question, to which Dennis's answer was to not ask stupid questions, then promptly continued his dialogue about the storage facility we had entered. The group laughed at his gruff honesty. Dennis pointed to the left and the group rotated in unison, following his pointed index finger, except for Ben, who kept his gaze glued on me.

My skin tingled with raised bumps that sent a chill down my legs, causing them to feel unsteady beneath my weight. I desperately wanted to walk to him, to ask him who he was and if he felt the consuming familiarity I did. I felt apprehensive out of guilt; there are cameras everywhere in Anexa's facilities, except for in Rob's office. I learned this when Rob and I first began dating because we always had to hurry back to his office to make love. The high-tech safety measures and number of security personnel needed at this new campus surprised me, but I came to understand the necessity because of the lethal poisons, infectious diseases, and organisms that were needed on site for pharmacological research and development. And then there was the intellectual property at the center of it all that also needed to be protected. The investment in developing and patenting a new commercially viable drug is astonishing.

I was never a cheater, it wasn't who I believed myself to be at my core, and I didn't want to give Rob any idea that I may be flirting with the idea. Guilt was thickly painted on my heart for even feeling the intense desire to know this man in the crowd.

I ducked my eyes away shyly when our eyes met again. The group moved forward on Dennis's command. Turning to look at Ben again, I was surprised to see he wasn't there. I anxiously searched the crowd, balancing on the tip of my toes and stretching my neck, wishing for at least one chance to say goodbye, but I couldn't find his face, until it appeared next me.

"Hi," his voice playful.

My body became a buoyant cluster of anxiety that I had no control over. I hadn't realized it, but I had stopped walking.

Did he see me looking for him? Embarrassment bloomed in my cheeks and my tongue dried as I stood in place gawking at his handsome face.

"Excuse me!" a posh woman in her sixties protested as she passed me in the crowd easing its way around me.

"We should probably…" Ben showed his infectious smile for the first time as he pointed ahead, hinting that I needed to move my feet. My face burned further with embarrassment.

We toddled next to each other, moving with the slow crowd. I avoided eye contact until I attempted to take control of my awkwardness. "Do I know you?"

"I don't think so," Ben answered as we crept along with the snail pace of the crowd, the corner of his eyes crinkling at me again.

Trembling with uncontrollable nervousness, I knew the only way to calm myself was to talk to him or walk away; talking to him made the trembling softer, more targeted, while walking away would stop it altogether.

I wanted more, so I elected to speak. "You're very familiar." I forcefully hid my smile like a foolish young girl with a crush.

He snickered at my question. "I've worked with your husband for years."

The smile I had been fighting forced its way across my face. I bit my lip to hide it and looked down at my black Miu Miu heels, concentrating on the shimmering black and gold gems.

Dennis asked loudly if there were any *good* questions, causing the group to snicker.

"Can I show you something?" he asked with quiet enthusiasm.

I nodded.

We let the crowd flow ahead of us, then moved to a door where Ben waved his security badge and after a beep and a thud, a green light flashed above the metal door. He led the way to another door, where he again waved his badge to be met by a green light and an unlocked door. Each time a door opened, the air being manipulated by the swinging door fanned his scent to me. His smell of sun-warmed skin and faint cologne deepened my breathing into quiet heavy inhales.

"This way," he said, walking into an empty lab that had yet to be furnished with equipment. I glanced up to the corners of the room and noticed only anchors where there would eventually be cameras. Unless someone saw us walk away together, no one knew where we were.

He stopped in the middle of the blindingly white room and held both arms out. "This…is mine."

"I see." I bit my lip again. "And what is 'this' exactly?"

"Well, it's not much now," he said, wiping the sparkling clean metal countertop with his fingertips, "but great minds will do great things here." He stepped closer to me. "My employees are engineering a neurotoxin for pain management to be distributed by Anexa, and here, right here, is where they'll create it." He stopped behind me and whispered into my ear, "Exciting, isn't it?" His warm breath on my ear forced my eyes shut. Each nerve in my legs and feet tingled with his proximity.

Stepping around to face me, my eyes opened to meet his. "Sophia—"

"Oh! Hello, Mr. Booth, Mrs. Claire," a surprised male voice announced himself.

"Hello, Larry," Ben and I replied in unison, greeting the security guard who had entered the unfinished laboratory.

Larry's round potbelly dared the buttons of his forest-green uniform to make it another moment. His thick glasses magnified eyes that shifted nervously between Ben and me.

"I wasn't sure who walked away from the group on the monitor. My apologizes." His mouth was left open as he breathed heavily, swaying from one foot to the other, turning towards the exit.

"Thank you, Larry," I said.

"We're almost done here," Ben declared as he winked at me.

Larry swayed once more, waddling out of the door, exiting the lab. The door beeped, locking behind him with a red light beaming above it.

"Can I see you again?" Ben asked with no smile. That was the first time I'd seen his face without a hint of a smile. His deep green eyes widened, made even more brilliant by his coffee-colored hair and black suit.

The room grew small and the air thick and hot. Gravity lessened, and it felt as if the floor had dropped out beneath me.

I wanted to know this person. This friend I'd never known.

"Sophia?" He offered a kind, comforting smile and moved closer. With his face just above mine, his pupils enlarged as his chest raised and fell quickly. He said, "I'll take anything you want to give. I just have to see you," his voice rough with determination.

I gripped the metal countertop behind me. As I leaned against it, I inhaled his scent. Our eyes locked on each other like two magnets strengthening as they grew closer together. I squeezed the countertop harder in anticipation.

"You're irresistible, Sophia. Do you feel time slowing?" he said with his lips almost touching mine. His breath warming my lips as he paused, his green eyes scanning mine intently, daring me to come to him. Daring me to press my lips against his.

It was at that moment I gave in to the overwhelming urge. That was the moment I became the woman I didn't think my faith would ever allow me to be—a cheater. I slowly leaned into him, pressing my lips to his soft, perfect lips that patiently waited for mine.

It was also the moment I gave another man the chance to hurt me. A man who said the same thing my husband had said when we first met—that he had an irresistible urge to know me and that time had slowed because of my presence. With Rob, I had felt the magnetism of lust, but with Ben, it was as if my soul had found something it left in another lifetime.

Eventually, I gave the friendly stranger all of me. Eventually, I fell hard for Benjamin Booth. Then, eventually, I realized bliss doesn't last.

Occasionally, I indulge myself in questioning what my life would be like if I had chosen Ben. He had said to me often, "I'll wait for you there alone," which is a lyric to a song and his way of saying he'd wait for me in any version of this life or the next. It was his way of saying, *I love you*; three words we never actually said out loud.

If I had chosen Ben, I'd have a family and possibly a real, loving marriage with a man who loves me, and only me. If I had chosen Ben, he wouldn't be a damaged, angry man set on loathing life and everyone in it.

10

What Remains

The clouds threaten lightning as we drive home from the airport. Few leaves still desperately hang onto their branches, not ready to give in to their end that comes with the changing season.

Walking into our home, Rob fades from me. Nothing was said. Nothing happened. I just feel it. A new energy courses through him, radiating dissatisfaction.

The ugly familiarity of my life slithers into place as we crawl into bed, saying nothing. It is, yet again, time to keep up the beautiful illusion of my life.

The morning is just as grey as yesterday evening. The greyness fills me, offering a strange comfort.

Rob went to the gym, then straight to work. He didn't even kiss me goodbye this morning. Guilt hangs sticky and demanding from inside me. I feel I have wronged him. The guilt slithers into sadness and I struggle through wanting to just disappear. I don't want to die. I just want to cease to exist.

I text him to receive some indication, some acknowledgement of love. Hovering, hoping, searching for a word or gesture that will bring my husband back to me.

Me: I love you.

Him: I love you, too.

Me: Come home for lunch?

Him: Sure.

I smile and let the butterflies fly freely in my belly.

After showering, I put my face on with expert skill and curl my hair. He always said he loves my hair when it's down and curled. I make lunch, planning for us to sit on the back porch to take advantage of possibly the last nice day this year. I'm looking forward to eating under the heat lamps in the crisp autumn afternoon.

When he arrives, he's arguing on his cellphone, talking business as usual. His shoulders raised to his ears, he grumbles spitefully into the phone. I motion for him to come out onto the porch where I have lunch waiting. He holds up his index finger in a hard, aggressive gesture.

My feelings are hurt.

I sit on the porch under the large stainless-steel heat lamp, waiting for him to finish his conversation, even though my stomach is gnawing on my spine, so we can eat together. He abruptly ends his conversation before rushing onto the porch and sitting at the table. He begins to eat briskly without saying a word.

"Anything I can help with?" I offer, anxiously spiraling

my wedding ring around and around and around my finger with the tip of my thumb, digging it painfully deep under my thumbnail.

He scoffs, "No." Answering with a full mouth and avoiding eye contact.

My gut tightens as I push my chest forward, reaching for every ounce of bravery in order to speak. I clear my throat quietly and say, "I was hoping to set a date with Tony…to have him prepare papers for the tasting room this week." I need Rob at this appointment with our attorney—he must sign the approval for the expenditure that he agreed to just days before in Maui.

He ignores me, glancing out at Deep River, and continues eating.

I glare at him, then sharply turn my head away, matching his gaze overlooking Deep River. I'm not sure if I turned to stop myself from saying something cutting, or to stop the tears from flowing. Without looking at him, keeping my eye on our view, I begin to speak. "We aren't doing the tasting room, are we?"

He takes plenty of time to chew his bite, swallow, then sip his drink. Clearing his throat, he says, "I just don't fancy the idea, Soph. They are rarely profitable, the market is oversaturated here, and you know nothing of the food industry." His voice is cold and indifferent, yet still mildly assertive, as it just was on the phone. His brown eyes never meet mine, instead keeping their gaze on his food as he delivers information he knows will hurt me.

I stand quickly, darting away. My eyes well with tears from the sadness bubbling in my chest. I don't want him to see his purposely hurtful words upset me.

Maui was a lie. He hasn't changed. He will never be who I need him to be. He will never allow me to have anything of my own; nothing that he doesn't have some control over. I lock myself in our bathroom and sob quietly.

I'm still young—I can leave now and start over, but my heart, my poor heart, was crucified years ago.

"Why?" I whisper to myself through the tears, honestly trying to find the answer to why I stay with this man. Somewhere in my desperation, the weight of my reality smacks me so hard that my breath labors through my tears. The prison I created for myself isn't made of anything tangible like bars or cement. Instead, mine is emotional and financial. A part of me stays because of financial comfort. If I divorce him, I'd get nothing due to the prenup I so happily signed; I foolishly thought he would give me what I needed, what I wanted. I thought I would get children and a loving marriage. I saw no harm in his legal requests.

I'd have to get a job, save, then move out. After his crying, negotiating, and begging didn't work, I'm sure he'd make it as difficult as possible once he knew I was really trying to leave him. He'd punish me both legally and emotionally.

I squeeze my eyes shut and raise my hands, placing my hands palm-to-palm. I rest them on my forehead and whisper aloud, praying for strength to stay or go, as silent tears fall from my cheeks.

If I didn't love him, it would be easier to stay and tolerate his bullshit. I'd be just like his mother: a woman who spent her life in an unhappy marriage in exchange for money and status.

Women like her care little for love.

Any sense of hope slips from me like water running through my fingers. I'm scared that once it's gone, I'll never acquire it again and I'll be stuck forever in this dark, miserable place.

I wish my love, like his, didn't last. I wish my heart didn't yearn for him and his attention. I'm full of resentment that coats any happiness I can muster like hot tar. I hate who he has turned me into. I'm so dependent upon him for love, attention, money, and validation. Maybe my love will fade in time, and I'll be left with only his financial comforts. I'd be so lucky.

I powder my nose, preparing to leave our bathroom that I've locked myself into. I secretly hope he will allow us to pass over this quarrel. And like with most things, we can move on without addressing it ever again.

Walking onto the back porch, I find his empty plate and glass, but no Rob. I search the house, then swing open the door to the garage.

His car is gone. He left.

He left me again. Broken hearted with his dirty dishes to clean.

I hate him.

I stay home for the day, swimming in a bottomless darkness that consumes me, ignoring all phone calls or texts. The pain of living with someone I love dearly who hurts me every day is becoming too much for my mind and body to manage. The pain of knowing he shares himself with other women. The anger that corrodes my stomach because of his controlling ways. The hatred of myself for allowing myself to be this woman floods me until nothing is left but a vast misery I cannot escape.

After cleaning the clutter from lunch and tidying the house—even though the housekeeper was here yesterday—I pour myself a glass of the wine Rob had created with a local vintner. I gulp it down, barely tasting the carefully crafted liquid.

It's now 8:30 p.m. and he still isn't home. I rest in our sitting room reading a book about a woman who fakes her death and attempts to frame her cheating husband. I should take notes.

I wait to hear the mudroom door open and close, signaling he's home. I don't dare text him; I don't think I can handle any further cruelty today.

It's now 10:30 p.m. and I'm drunk. So drunk I can no longer focus on the words in my book.

I hear the door to the garage close as he strolls in, tall and with purpose.

"It's ten. You could have called," I say, thick with aggravation, as he walks silently past me on his way to our bedroom.

"Sorry, I got caught up," he says, keeping his stride towards our bedroom.

"Hey!" I stand, and the vertical position makes my head increasingly murky with wine. Anger burns a white-hot fire in my chest. It slithers up my throat, reaching my tongue, then my mouth fires drunk words. "Don't you think I deserve more respect than this?"

"What?" he arrogantly huffs, stopping and hesitantly turning his large body towards me.

"I'm your wife, Robert. I'm your wife! How would you feel if I didn't call and came home whenever I liked? How would that make you feel?" I spit my words at him and drunkenly wobble closer.

"Are you drunk?" he asks, his face twisting with conceited judgment.

"Don't discount my words! You can't do this to me any longer. I won't tolerate it!" I yell through tears that escape without my permission, and then I smell it. He smells of sweet sweat. The smell that intoxicates me during and after we make love. Then, women's floral perfume hits my nostrils like a starting pistol, and I lunge at him.

"I fucking hate you! I hate you! Who was it tonight, you fucking asshole?" My fists fire sloppily at him and he catches each pitiful attempt. He twists me around, holding me tightly, creating a straitjacket with his arms.

"Shhh," he hisses in my ear, but I continue to sob uncontrollably. "I'm sorry. I love you. I'm sorry," his voice now soft and kind. My knees buckle, and I fall back into him, allowing the protective blanket of hate wrapped around my heart to fall.

"Why?" I ask through my sobbing.

I'm broken. This is a new darkness I didn't know existed. Its mass too heavy for my body as it slouches further to the ground.

"Shhh, I love you." He turns me to face him, then kisses me. I let him. I melt into him and we collapse together on the floor. I gain control of my tears, slowing my sobs.

"I can't do this anymore," I murmur with honesty. It's true. My heart can't handle this man any longer.

My body draped over his, my legs straddling him on the hallway's wooden floor as he holds me like a child being carried to bed. He reaches for my face, cupping it in between his hands, and he kisses me again, crashing his lips deeply into mine.

"I love you. I'm sorry." He begs between his rough kisses. "I don't want anyone but you."

He reaches for my top and quickly pulls it over my head. I stand hurriedly, and he rises just as quickly. His large hands cup my head again and he forces another aggressive kiss from me.

I yell, "Stop!" into his mouth, breaking away by placing my palms firmly against his chin and pressing upwards with great effort.

"I hate you!" I shout, striking him across the face, causing his head to jolt sideways. The strike does nothing but provoke him and sting my palm.

He comes at me fiercely. Kissing me powerfully, grabbing at me so roughly that my skin burns where he touches.

I push away and strike him again. "NO!" I shriek through frantic tears.

He tosses his tie over his left shoulder, then bends at his knees, picking me up easily. He tosses me over his right shoulder, then marches down the hallway towards our bedroom. Storming inside, he hurls me onto the impeccably made bed, and with one tug of my ankle, he is on top of me, kissing me through my whimpers. Threading his fingers through mine, he holds my arms above my head, pressing them into the mattress.

"I love you," he whispers repeatedly as he presses gentle kisses to my lips. "Please. I love you," he whispers between supple kisses on my neck. With one hand gripping both of my wrist together, holding my arms above my head still, the other searches between my thighs until he finds my opening.

"I love you," he says with his chest heaving deeply. His fingers slowly rocking me into oblivion, gently persuading me to give in to him, as his mouth swallows my moans.

The power this man has over me will kill.

11

The Moon and the Tower

My eyes burn from the late morning sunlight bouncing off everything white in my bedroom. I reach over to Rob's side of the bed only to find a jumble of white sheets where his muscular body should be.

My phone dings, alerting me to a text message.

Stretching my stiff legs through the messy sheets and pointing my toes, I reach for my cellphone resting on my nightstand. Wiggling my body back under the warmth of the blankets, I turn the side of my face on my pillow, allowing me to view the text message.

Ben: Sophia I'm sorry. Call me now, please. Need to talk ASAP.

I delete it.

I don't shower; I have no energy for it. Instead, I sloppily place my hair up in a French bun and place minimal makeup on, attempting to hide the blue crescents under my hazel eyes and the deepening hollows of my cheeks. I then select my favorite church dress. The Valentino dress I bought to be my Sunday church dress years ago has continued to be a staple for Mass and other church services. Its long, navy-colored sleeves cover my wrists that display bruises from where Rob had clutched tightly last night. It hangs faintly from my body, as to not show my curves, and its pleated crepe length sits inches below my knees to remain modest and respectful. The crystal-embroidered peter pan collar sits high at my neck, but expresses a feminine sparkle with the pink, blue, and green crystals.

I head to Rob's side of the closet and open the top drawer of his dresser. I select one of the five bankrolls resting among other trinkets spread messily throughout the drawer. I yank a single bill out, not bothering to look at the denomination. I place my neatly folded white chapel veil in my clutch and shove the bill into the unzipped internal pocket of the clutch. After putting my shoes on, I walk to the kitchen to collect my keys. The clock on the kitchen wall tells me that it's two thirty, and I feel as if time has sneakily slipped passed me again. If it weren't for my cellphone, I doubt I'd even know what day it is.

I had lain alone in bed for hours this morning after Rob left. My body too heavy to move, my mind to numb to think.

I arrive at church, parallel parking on the main street in front of the towering brick building instead of parking in the lot dedicated to the church. Glancing in my rearview mirror before opening my door, I see an unmarked police vehicle parked behind me. The license plate displaying "XMT" vertical to the plate numbers, proving that it is a government vehicle.

I step out of my car, adjusting my dress. My heels crunch the fallen leaves from the tall, aged trees surrounding St. Mary's Catholic Church. Striding up the concrete steps, I reach the tall ornate wooden door and pull on the enormous brass handle.

The smell of this old church reminds me of my grandmother; both smell of a time that has passed yet somehow still lingers in the present. The smell makes me miss her terribly. Walking into the church, I immediately feel like a child again, walking together with Cassidy down the aisle to find our favorite pew. We were to never run, always walk "like a young lady," our mother would remind us. Like the child I was, I look for my favorite pew, which is the fifth pew from the front, on the left. The church is empty other than the custodian who is changing a light bulb in a sconce fixed to a thick pillar.

I slide into the fifth pew, looking ahead at the altar surrounded by flowers and covered in a white lace runner with the Blessed Virgin Mary statue standing next to it. I reach into my clutch, unfolding my veil, then place it upon my head carefully as to not disturb my hair. I glance over at the confessional booths, noticing that the doors are closed. I gaze up at the walls above the altar, studying the painting of two angels, both holding sashes that display Latin I do not understand. To the left of each painted angel are pristine windows that tell the story of Christ through exquisitely detailed stained-glass, each color placed precisely.

I adjust my weight on the solid wood of the pew, lean my head back as I close my eyes, then exhale slowly through my mouth as my shoulders release tension I wasn't aware they were holding. I hear the confessional doors open and footsteps echo off the walls and tiled floors. My eyes remain closed as I grasp at the slight release this moment brings, desperate for even a moment of peace.

"Mrs. Claire?" A woman's voice breaks through my coveted silence. I crack open one eye, leaving my head tilted back. Detective Cruz is standing before me in her grey pantsuit. "Hello," she says with a smile that narrowly moves her lips.

I shift quickly, moving my head and shoulders to face her, opening both eyes. "Hello, detective," I say with a slight bow of my head.

"Would you mind if I join you?" she asks. I pause and seriously consider if I would mind. She pushes, "Only for a moment."

I uncross my legs and scoot over. Trusting that my annoyance isn't splashed across my face. I lift my clutch, moving it to the other side of me. She sits down gracefully, then crosses her legs. I exhale the irritation bubbling beneath my surface and look over at her with a forced, tight smile. It's the first time I've seen her with her hair down. Her black hair left untamed with its thick natural curls falling over her shoulders.

"I'm sorry to intrude. I was just in confession and saw you here."

"No intrusion," I say, and add a polite smile.

"I've been coming here since I was a little girl. It still smells the same." She giggles as she waves her hand in front of her nose.

"I don't mind the smell. It's comforting in a strange way," I answer.

"Funny how a smell can bring you straight back to a moment

in time."

We sit in awkward silence. Our eyes straight ahead. I adjust my hands in my lap, intertwining my fingers together as I wait for her to start asking questions about Rob, but she doesn't.

"I was going to light a candle for my sister." She breaks the silence and points her tiny, unmanicured brown hand towards the altar filled with mostly unlit candles. She looks into my eyes, her face soft and kind. I want to ask her about what I read online about her sister, her mother, her past, but before any of the questions can form in my mind, her dark eyes meet mine and she offers, "It was a long time ago."

I reply with one short nod. "I'd like to light one, too," I add.

She stands, swiping her palms down the front of her suit pants, brushing away any wrinkles from sitting. "Shall we?" She raises her arm in the direction of the altar that holds the votive candles. I stand, much taller than her in my heels, as she waits for me to walk in front of her, then follows closely behind. The altar isn't far, but walking with her behind me makes it feel like a mile.

At the altar, we both reach for a match. She goes for the fourth unlit candle, and I stretch for the fifth. We strike our matches at the same time; her wick catches before mine and she rests her candle back on the altar. My wick catches and I place it fifth in line on the altar. As we both kneel and silently pray, I realize the woman next to me isn't the detective investigating my husband. The woman kneeling next to me is Adella Cruz.

She stands first, immediately making the sign of the cross.

Still kneeling, I whisper, "I love you. I'm sorry." Standing to my feet, I make the sign of the cross, then lift my mother's cross to my lips and kiss it, releasing it to fall freely at my chest.

"You okay?" Adella asks me.

"Yes, why?" I ask, then feel a tear roll down my cheek. I wipe it away and reassure her that I'm okay.

"So, there's a deli right around the corner. It's owned by friends of my family. Would you like to join me for a quick bite?" she asks playfully.

"I'd like that," I answer, expecting the line of questioning to happen there. Maybe she felt uncomfortable conducting business here. Maybe Detective Cruz will show up at the deli.

I remove the veil from my head carefully, neatly folding it. I open my Bulgari clutch, pinch the bill I took from Rob's drawer—which I notice is a one-hundred-dollar bill—then place the white veil into the pocket that held the money. Once I close my clutch, I fold the bill precisely, then smoothly slip it into the donation box next to the candle altar. Adella reaches into her back pocket where she retrieves a black leather monogrammed wallet. She, too, reaches for a one-hundred-dollar bill and crams it into the donation box. For a moment, I wonder why she would donate such a large amount for someone on a detective's salary. But then I remember she is an heir to a small fortune left by her mother. My infatuation for her deepens.

Walking to the deli, the crisp autumn air nips at my uncovered skin. A street performer sits ahead. Her long greyish-brown hair hangs tangled and dirty. An unfolded cardboard box sits on the sidewalk in front of her as she rolls dice bearing symbols unknown to me, talking aloud to herself. A brown dog sits unbothered by her side. As we get closer, the dog begins barking, staying seated on its hind legs as we are readying to pass.

"You," she points at me, causing us to stop in front of the woman. "Sirius has something to tell you." She motions to the brown dog who now sits in silence, wagging its tail so intensely that his entire backside sways side to side.

My first thought is that I don't have any more cash on me to donate. The second is to berate myself for stopping.

"Well, hello, fancy lady. Dice aren't for you. No, no, no. No dice. No dice. You are a card seeker," she rattles off quickly as she sets the dice to the side. Her dirty hands reach inside an army green duffle bag that rests on the sidewalk next to her. I glance over at Adella, who is smiling, thoroughly enjoying my discomfort in this moment. She gives a teasing wink.

I tuck my clutch into the nook of my armpit, then cross my arms over my chest, digging my nails into the skin that hides under my navy-blue sleeves.

She shuffles some cards in her dirty hands with impressive ease, counting to five. Then extends the deck to me. "Pick a card," she commands, and I notice she's missing many teeth.

I oblige, reaching out my manicured fingers with chipped red polish. The autumn breeze picks up and rustles the yellow leaves on the trees above us. Some fall around us to the wet concrete.

"The Moon card, in reverse," she announces to her audience of two. She piles the cards together and looks at the bottom of the deck, showing the card to us. "And the Tower is on the bottom." She glances between Adella and me, and I wonder if that was it. Show's over?

"Are you a Pisces?" she asks me.

"Yes. March seventh," I answer with one brow raised, speculating about what kind of con this is.

"Thank you," Adella says as she tosses a ten-dollar bill on the woman's cardboard mat. She grips my arm, pulling me away from the woman and her dog.

"That was weird," Adella says to me, placing some distance between us and the woman.

I glance back at her as she yells, "The Tower is coming for you! There's no stopping it. And what is done in the darkness of moonlight will come to light!" then begins laughing and petting the dog, who savors the attention.

Adella sits in the deli, slumped over her pastrami on rye, chewing aggressively, as I daintily sip a warm cup of tea. I think about how my tower had already fallen. I'm sitting in the rubble, desperately trying to make sense of my new life. A life where the woman sitting across from me thinks my husband is a murderer yet hasn't mentioned it once.

"Mrs. Claire." Adella wipes her mouth with her napkin and takes a pull from her straw. I push my shoulders back and lift my chin, waiting for her line of questioning to begin. Detective Cruz has arrived. "Who was your candle for? Your parents?" she asks unapologetically.

I shake my head. "I was pregnant," I answer honestly as I place my lips to the small teacup and sip its warmth while maintaining eye contact.

Silence. Adella is noticeably thrown. She looks at the cross that hangs from my neck, then back to my eyes. "That must have been incredibly difficult for you and Robert," she manages to say.

"It wasn't Rob's baby. I had an affair. He doesn't know." There's no point in hiding this from her. If she digs deep enough, for long enough, she'll find out.

She sits frozen, her gaze delving deeper into mine. I can tell her center is off balance around me, and this information has served as a final blow. Checkmate.

She pushes her plate aside and leans back in her chair. "Do you know much about his life outside of your marriage? His work, hobbies, his…" She trails off.

"His other women?" I finish for her. "It's okay, you can say it. I don't know what I don't know, and I like it that way." I sip my tea with my eyes still locked on her, watching her attempt to maneuver through this conversation.

"Just like he doesn't know what he doesn't know?" she adds. "Who did you have the affair with?"

"Does it matter?" I challenge her, setting my teacup down.

"Not at this juncture, no. I'm simply curious." A blush fans across her cheeks, making the tiny scars on her cheeks more prominent.

I slide my empty teacup to the side of the small tabletop. I lean over the table and rest my chin on my left palm, searching her face for answers, attempting to decipher every flicker of her eyes.

She cracks her neck, stretching it slowly from one side to the other, then leans over her hands resting on the tabletop. She gives me a quizzical look.

Her strength fails her as her face breaks into a flushed smile and she glances away. She returns her eyes to mine, wary and uncertain.

I notice a bandage on her hand and reach for it, cupping her hand between mine. "What happened?" I ask as I caress her hand delicately, noticing her unmanicured nails that have all been bitten down to nubs. She allows me to manipulate her hand as she watches my face, ignoring my question. She slowly returns the caress until our fingers gracefully slide together, locking with each other. I pull away, then glide back in slowly, savoring the sensualism in something so simple.

"Who did you cheat on your husband with?" Adella asks again.

"Why does it matter?" I challenge her again as I continue to stroke her fingers within mine.

The server comes to our table and sets the bill face down on the table. "I'm only charging you for the sandwich, Adella," the teenage girl says. Adella pulls away from me and puts cash on the bill, handing it to the teen. "Keep the change, Jazzy," Adella says over her shoulder to the teen as she walks away from our table.

"It matters. I find myself worrying because you're still in the house with him. It matters because your husband is a suspect in a murder case, and I need to know what Robert's motives might be. It just matters, Sophia," she says as she stands. "Just be careful," she fumes as she hastily shoves her arms into her jacket. I feel her pull away again and insert unseen space between us.

I stand to meet her and just as I open my mouth in an attempt to bring her back to me, she turns swiftly for the door. Stopping at the door, with her back to me and one hand on the doorknob, her shoulders slouch as she tilts her head up in thought. She lets out a sharp exhale then swings the door open and walks through it.

With my mouth agape, I sink back in my chair and a powerlessness of confusion washes over me as I glance at her empty chair. I look around the deli only to see that I'm completely alone. Over my left shoulder I spot a large palette knife painting hanging on the wall. It reminds me of artwork by Paul Cèzanne, an artist from the 19th century I studied in college. The gold frame coated in a thick layer of dust but the painting itself appears to be well cared for.

The painting displays a little girl wearing a navy-blue dress that stops just below her knees and a diamond necklace dangles from her extended right hand, presenting it to the viewer. Her brown hair pulled back away from her face, reminding me of my own today. She's barefoot standing in a field of brown grass with clouds behind her that are so grey they're almost black. I stare at what should be her face but it's awash with varying nudes and browns, as if smudged on purpose. She's surrounded by black wolves that are just as tall as she. Their yellow eyes not on her, but on the viewer, and their ears upright and alert.

I glance down at my sleeves and back at the painting, confirming that my dress is the same color as the little girl in the painting. I swallow hard and my jaw clenches. Among the wolves, one hides directly behind her, blending with the dark gray clouds. Its yellow eyes pop against its black fur and of all the wolves, it's the only one revealing a fierce sneer.

"Did you want anything else? Another cup of tea, maybe?" The servers asks as she removes Adella's empty plate from the table.

"No, thank you, Jazzy" I stand, unable to remove my eyes from the painting of the little girl among the wolves. I eye the fangs of the wolf standing behind the little girl and my legs grow heavy.

"It's Jasmine," she says with a friendly smile that I notice out of the corner of my eye. "Adella and I grew up together... I mean, our families did. Jazzy is a nickname and not one I love. But then again, how often do we like our nicknames?" She giggles as she reaches for my empty cup. "My brother's nickname is way worse."

I hear her continue to talk, but I'm unable to respond even though my brain is shouting at me to offer a polite response, to socially perform as I normally would. Instead, I collect my purse from the table and step backwards while maintaining my eyes on the wolves and the little girl in the navy-blue dress with no face. My hip bumps against a table, knocking over a saltshaker.

"Thank you," I muster, flashing a glance at Jasmine then rush towards the front door, jerking it open with haste then thrusting myself out into the cool autumn air, far away from the girl in the blue dress among wolves.

12

For What It's Worth

After parking and gathering myself, I rush into the crowd. I'm twenty minutes late for my appointment. I'm never late. Opening the large glass door to Chanel, I'm greeted immediately by a charismatic gentleman in a black, classic fit suit. His sandy brown hair is styled impeccably, and his suit tailored to his thin frame perfectly. He apologizes for not opening the door as I rush past him. The music muffles my heels slightly as I walk towards the private room where I always meet my saleswoman. The store is clean, bright, and always smells of florals. I pass a beautiful woman dressed in a cream-colored pantsuit with her black hair pulled back into a classic low bun. She delicately sifts through the neat and inviting ready-to-wear racks. Just before I walk through an open door that leads to the back of the store, she turns to look at me, and our eyes meet as I search for recognition in an unfamiliar face. Walking into the private room, it feels as if I've stepped into a living room. The decor offers elegant, crisp taste appealing to most clientele. I set my tote down on the coffee table, but before I'm able to sit, I'm greeted by my saleswoman, Georgie.

"Well, hello, darling," Georgie says with her lovely French accent and a kiss on the cheek. "Cappuccino or champagne today?" Her freshly lifted face offers a tight, unnatural smile.

"May I have a water, please?"

"Still or sparkling?"

"Still, no ice, please."

Georgie's assistant leaves to fetch my water as Georgie shuts the door behind her.

"So, darling, how are you?" she asks as she reaches for my hands, lifting them to the space between us.

"I'm well. How are you?" I give her velvety, vaguely aged hands a squeeze.

"I'm absolutely fantastic. I just got back from Paris, visiting family, and I met my newest grandbaby, Alice." She beams with pride.

"Oh, that's wonderful. Do you have pictures?" I ask politely.

"Oh, of course! But first, we need to get you into your dress. It arrived yesterday and I had them call you immediately! It's enchanting, really." She claps with delight.

I giggle at her excitement about everything and anything. She leaves the room to fetch the dress I purchased a month ago for my upcoming charity event.

Before Rob, I had never experienced the luxury of haute couture, let alone my own private suite. My parents were both professors and taught us to live within our means. My father, who specialized in economics, had always cautioned us to use credit responsibly, to save before spending, and to plan for everything, including salary expectations after college. He was an intelligent and honest man, my father, but he held rigid views that still gnaw at me, causing a ping of guilt when spending.

It was so ingrained in me to feel guilty about money. But after a few years as Robert's wife, I learned to enjoy the mere thought of his face twisted in surprise when seeing the Centurion Card statement.

Georgie strolls in, behind her the assistant with my water. Both women dressed in all black, classically accessorized. Georgie rolls the dress form to the middle of the room while holding the length in her hand. She stops, allowing its sweeping shades of black silk chiffon to cascade to the floor. The bodice filled by the mannequin's form highlights the extraordinary details of the fitted ruched bustier. The shimmery halter straps continue down the front, cupping just under the bust. Both women gasp in wonderment as Georgie turns on the display light above it. The light further brings out the various shades of black.

"Well?" Georgie says, anticipating my excitement.

"It's beautiful." I smile while eyeing the dress, thinking how much this will cost Rob.

"We'll leave you. Push the button when you're ready for us to join you," Georgie says.

I set my water down on the coffee table and saunter to the dress, reaching out to feel the fabric. I draw the silk chiffon between my fingers, careful not to snag it on my nails. The sensation reminding me of my Zuhair Murad wedding gown.

I had dreamed of an off-the-shoulder, beaded brocade mermaid wedding gown. No designer name needed. It's what I had always pictured since I was a little girl. But Robert's mother vetoed it immediately, calling it tacky in the most casual, repugnant manner. She then suggested I go with a more sophisticated style that would remain timeless for generations to come, promptly sending a representative from Zuhair Murad to have me fitted. While my final dress was beautiful, my ability to choose was taken and I was upset. To comfort me, Robert sought to explain his mother's behavior. "She would be this way with anyone, Soph. Please don't take it personally," he had said. His words stuck with me. To me they meant I could be anyone; it's about filling the space at Robert's side, and something so personal as my wedding dress was not personal. To them, a wedding was a business transaction. An event to showcase one's success. An optimal place to deepen business relationships. I don't look back on my wedding day like most women do. What should be fond memories of a day filled with love is stained by the realization that came years later; I was merely a space-filler at my own wedding.

Pressing the button to signal to Georgie, I hold the bodice to my chest so that it stays until she zips the back. Georgie knocks once, then enters. Upon seeing me, she claps again with enthusiasm.

"Magnifique." Georgie gleams as she rushes to me, zipping the enclosure with ease.

I turn to face the full-length mirror, allowing my arms to fall now that the dress is secure. The dress was fitted for my body, hugging each curve as it should. I notice a gap at the bust and before I can address it, Georgie eyes the gap, turns swiftly, then strides across room. She opens the top drawer of a wooden dresser in the corner of my suite, waving her hand elegantly through the air as she determines which item to select. She pulls something out of the drawer and walks back to me. "Here, my darling. We all need a little help from time to time." Georgie winks at me, handing me silicone bra inserts. "It's nature's cruel joke that us women always loose it there first," she adds.

I manage a faltering smile and reach for the inserts. I'm thankful she doesn't comment on my weight loss but instead glosses over it to find a solution. I lean forward, sliding in each insert, then stand upright.

"Voilà!" Georgie waves one hand through the air with a smile. The wrinkles around her eyes are always most prominent when she is sincerely happy. "You're exquisite, my darling. Simply stunning."

"Thank you, Georgie. Really. This is perfect for the event."

"You said you have shoes for the event, yes?"

"Yes. I won't need a clutch either. It's perfect," I say as I turn away from her, signaling for her to unzip me. I turn my head and quietly ask, "Oh, and will you please bring me a glass of champagne? I'd like to browse for a bit." As soon as she unzips me, she excuses herself, allowing me privacy to step out of the dress and change back into my clothes. I hear her heels just outside the door, so instead of pressing the button, I simply open the door for her to come in once I finish.

"For you, my darling. I keep your favorite on hand *just for you*," Georgie says as she passes me the flute filled with champagne.

"Thank you! I so rarely drink Bollinger because Rob dislikes it," I say as I take a sip, savoring its zest dancing across my tongue. Sauntering to the charcoal-colored velvety couch, I set my glass down next to my purse, then sit down, slipping on my sapphire suede pumps. Georgie quickly gathers the dress to box it. "Georgie?" I say to her as I stand, holding my tote in one hand and champagne in the other. "Thank you," I say as I walk towards her, truly meaning it. Being here is my escape, and Georgie never wants, asks, or pushes. Being here is easy. Being here, I can relax.

"Of course, my dear. It's always my pleasure. I'll have this waiting for you up front and Rudy will place it in your car when you're ready," she says, referring to the gentleman who greeted me when I arrived.

We walk out of the room together, and as she turns to package the dress that will cost Rob a small fortune, I continue towards the boutique where the music grows louder.

When my champagne is almost gone, I set the flute and my tote down on nearby glass shelving, reaching in to find my favorite red Chanel lipstick. Using the mirrored wall, I reapply my smudged lipstick. The woman I passed while walking back to my suite is still shopping, and she too is drinking champagne. Our eyes meet and I offer a polite smile, but her face remains frozen as she takes a sip of champagne.

As the champagne settles, I grow sluggish and I'm ready to leave having found nothing else to charge. I begin walking to the front of the store and notice the light outside is now gone, having given in to nightfall. This time of year plays sly tricks with daylight. As I walk past the beautiful, unfriendly woman,

I mentally curse myself for not bringing my coat in with me as I know it will be a chilly walk to my car.

"Your husband must like Passion," the woman says to me as I pass her. Still no expression on her face.

"Excuse me?" I stop, turning towards her.

"Your lipstick shade. Is it not Chanel's Passion?"

"It's Pirate, actually." I offer a playful grin, then add, "Very similar reds."

"Yes. I guess I can get away with Passion…with my complexion."

"You have a beautiful complexion," I offer.

"Thanks," she snaps. "Most men see my complexion and features and assume I'm the embodiment of some submissive fantasy they've always dreamed of."

"Why do they assume that?" I ask, glancing around us nervously, knowing I may regret delving deeper into this bizarre conversation. I see Georgie near the front of the store speaking with another customer.

"Because I'm Filipino." Her dark, perfectly almond-shaped eyes remain on me, barely blinking. She sets her flute down on the glass table between us, walking towards me. "Well, Filipino American," she adds as she stops in front of me. Her silver diamond drop earrings continue to sway from her movement and her crisp, clean perfume floats around us.

"You're gorgeous," I say politely, desperately wanting to get out of this conversation.

She stares at me without blinking.

"Have a wonderful evening," I say, stepping to the side. I attempt to walk around her towards the front where Georgie and my dress wait, but she steps with me, blocking my path. We stand face-to-face, and she still says nothing. I put my arms down to my sides, gripping the handle of my tote in one hand.

"Excuse me!" I'm tired, hungry, and I want to go home.

"I always wondered what you looked like up close. I get the appeal now," she says as her eyes pore over my face.

"I have to go." I shove her with my shoulder, pushing past her. I don't have the patience for this.

The volume of her voice swells as she says, "Looking back at our affair, at all of his promises, I don't think it was ever going to end any other way. You won. He'll always choose you." She shrugs her shoulders.

I stop, turning on my heels. "What?" I spit.

"But," she continues as she steps closer, "I think it was Ann Landers who said, 'If you marry a man who cheats on his wife, you'll be married to a man who cheats on his wife,' and who wants that?" she mocks me. "Tell Robert that Fiona says hello," she says, and for the first time, her eyes change, squinting in a hateful glare.

My stomach drops and my head becomes dizzy. I regret drinking the champagne on an empty stomach. I stalk away from her as quickly as I can with my head spinning and heart thumping. My vision tunnels but I manage to stumble my way to Georgie, whose face is plastered with worry.

"Oh, darling, what's the matter?" She moves quickly, reaching for my arm.

I'm hot. So hot that my body feels wet and clothes sticky. The room spins as I grip Georgie's arm.

I crave the cool air outside. I must get outside.

I turn to walk towards the door, using a nearby display of scarves to keep me upright. My tote falls from my arm and I hear Georgie's voice next to me. Her blurry body reaches for my tote on the floor, collecting the items that have fallen out.

I feel like I might explode from the heat as the spinning accelerates, and as I open my mouth to ask Georgie to help me get outside, vomit escapes instead of words. The light vanishes from my vision and my body slumps to the tiled floor.

I open my eyes to Chanel's brightly lit interior. The scent of the store that normally soothes me is now overpowering and gives me an instant headache.

"Oh, darling. Are you okay?" Georgie's voice breaks through the collection of muffled conversations.

My right shoulder and head throb, and I have a sour taste in my mouth. "Yes, I believe so," I answer her, and attempt to sit up. I extend my hand, using the floor to push my torso upwards, but it slips in wetness, causing me to fall back to the floor. I close my eyes, gathering every ounce of strength I have left to sit up. I open my eyes and use my elbows to boost myself up onto my bottom in one swift movement. I look up, glancing at the worried faces surrounding me. I look to Georgie, who is holding my tote. "I'll take that, Georgie. Thank you," I say, attempting to gain control.

"Oh, no, darling. Olivia is fetching something for you," she says as she points down at my hands, both covered in my own vomit. I'm dripping in my own vomit. "It's safe with me, dear," Georgie adds.

After much negotiation, no one at the store called the paramedics. After further negotiations, Georgie instructed

Rudy to place my well-packaged dress in my car, then they let me drive myself home.

Upon arriving home, I strip down to nothing, placing my vomit-soaked clothes and shoes in a black garbage bag. I leave it by the door to throw in the can before Rob comes home, but a shower is crucial. Naked, I hurry to the bathroom, turning the shower knob as hot as it permits. While I wait for the scorching hot water, I look in the mirror and am horrified. My hair is crisp with dried vomit that I fell in, my eye makeup smeared under my eyes from sweating profusely, and my treasured red lipstick smeared across the bottom half of my face.

"You left Chanel looking like this," I chastise my reflection.

Stepping into the steamy shower, the water pours over my head, saturating my crispy hair. I exhale loudly, releasing some tension from my humiliating experience. *Fucking Fiona,* I think.

For what it's worth, I am the one who won. But he's not the prize I thought I was winning.

13

Open House

Standing at my kitchen counter, gazing out over Deep River, I scroll through Facebook on my cellphone. I find Rob had checked into the gym about two hours ago, complete with a selfie of him and Abe Brown on the basketball court. I don't mind him spending time with Abe, he's a good man—a self-made man. Recently, Abe has spent a great amount of time with Rob, helping Anexa acquire another company.

I continue scrolling, my mind is infected quickly with dread when I come across an article from the *Deep River Herald* that mentions another murder that took place last night. The headline reads, "Another Woman Killed. Police Scramble for Answers." The short article describes the death as matching the other victims and shares her name, Abby Usher, and her photograph. She is beautiful and young, just like the others. I examine her, studying her glossy red hair, button nose, and porcelain skin.

Guilt at the death of another young woman pulses through my veins, followed by a crushing anxiety. My phone falls from my hand, tumbling to the kitchen counter as my body grows heavy with my eyes fixed open. I want to cry but the numbness created by a strange cocktail of sensations won't allow tears to form. I assume the detectives will be contacting me again, and soon.

I float to our bedroom and crawl under the covers. Closing my eyes, allowing the satisfaction of sleep to slowly slide over me. The peaceful break from my bizarre reality is welcomed until I'm interrupted by the quiet hum of Rob's car pulling slowly into the garage.

I wait to hear him. The door to the garage closes loudly and he makes his way to our bedroom, playing noisily with his keys.

I close my eyes, pretending I'm asleep before he makes it to our bedroom.

A tickle dances on my nose, causing me to open my eyes abruptly to find him above me, kissing my forehead.

"Hi," he whispers.

I moan, still pretending to be sleepy.

"I need to shower and get ready to go. Will you drive me to the airport?" he asks, hovering over me.

"Yes, of course." I sit up lazily to watch him walk to the bathroom and undress, tossing his dirty gym clothes to the hamper and missing. I don't have plans today, but it would be nice if he would have planned my driving him to the airport sooner than thirty minutes before leaving.

He says something from the shower, but I can't make out

his words from our bed. I pitch the heavy down blanket off my naked body and walk to the shower where Rob stands scrubbing his face.

Something that always annoyed me about this man: he would be on the opposite side of the house, yet assume it is my job to come to him to hear what he has to say. Yet, if I needed to speak to him, it was my job to walk to him so he could hear me. A twinge of anger simmers in my chest as I stand at the open marble shower watching him.

"What?" I ask, placing sharpness on the question to showcase my annoyance.

"I'll be back on Tuesday. I really wish you'd come," he mutters through the scrubbing of his hair, as steam billows in my face.

He doesn't want me to come. He never does. He would only say this when he knew I couldn't or didn't want to. When I wanted to, he would create a reason why I couldn't come. I know what he does on his business trips. My lips purse remembering early in our marriage when I would accompany him. We would sneak back to our hotel room any chance we got to make love. Even after everything, I still miss that man. The naked man in front of me is a shell of who that man was. I turn away as my eyes well with tears and quickly move to the sink, splashing water on my face.

After a quiet ride to the airport, I pull into the loading/unloading area, then step out of my car to see him off.

"Win big in Vegas," I murmur.

"You know these conferences are never fun. I'll be lucky if I have a second to stop at a slot machine."

Fucking liar, I think, offering him a forced smile.

He leans in, squeezes me, and says quietly, "Have fun with Melanie tonight."

I put little effort into returning his hug. He presses his lips against mine and I try not to cringe. I wave goodbye as he disappears inside the crowded airport.

I had completely forgotten about dinner with Melanie. My mind is so cluttered with dread and doubts, creating bubbles of vertigo in my memory.

I let out a giggle at the absurdity of pretending everything is okay. But it will be okay; it has to be. The man Detective Cruz described doesn't exist in my home. I'm sure she thinks I'm too close to him to see him clearly, though.

I'm home from the airport quickly—the drive a blur. I'm vibrating with agitation. My heart races as I bolt into the house. Jogging to the bedroom, I head straight to his dresser in our closet. I fumble through the drawer with his gym shorts and move on to the next drawer, then the next and the next. My body moving impossibly fast, but the adrenaline has frozen time. I dig in each pocket of every shirt, pants, and suit. My body sails to the laundry basket and dumps it over, frantically burrowing through its contents.

I stop suddenly.

I don't even know what I am looking for. I've never done this before. I've never been *this* woman. I look down at his dirty underwear laying over my bent knee and begin to sob, curling into a ball on the plush rug sprawled on our closet floor. My mind is slipping from my control, or at the very least, I'm losing the sense of self I once proudly owned.

Peeling myself from the rug to sit up, I notice the mess I made for the first time. I begin to pick up, placing each item where it belongs. Placing a shoe back on its rack, I see a crumpled paper in his tiny oval garbage can.

Could he be that dumb? I think.

Plucking the paper from the garbage, I unfold it and see it's only an advertisement for an open house. The house isn't anything he would purchase. He likes to think he is an investor in real estate, being an owner of a few rentals, but this isn't his style. He likes newer, cheap, lower income homes. This is a split-level from the 1970s located in Prosser, about a half hour from us. He hates Prosser. The heading boasts, "The Alternative Lifestyle."

I stare at the flyer in my hands, sitting on the thickly tufted cream bench I so carefully chose for this space. There are no interior photographs, only one exterior. A strange symbol displayed top and center of the flyer strikes me; the flyer has the same symbol on the pin I found in Rob's office the night of the trespasser. The symbol made of a pyramid created with one thick black line, with another thick black line creating an infinity symbol running vertical through it. The same symbol I found in Maui carved into the wood post. Below the symbol, the flyer states that this evening's open house is invite only, with a start time of 9 p.m. and no end time listed. I crumple the flyer back into a tight wad, then toss it back into the small garbage can.

I finish placing everything back into its designated place. My body and mind slowly grow clear and stable. A clarity only a good cry can bring.

The clock on the wall warns me I'm to meet Melanie in an hour.

After showering and perfecting my makeup, I place my hair in a high ponytail and stare at my finished work in the mirror. My cheek bones protrude from my normally round face and the blue crescents under my eyes peek through the concealer I've carefully placed. I wonder if Melanie will notice.

The crumpled paper radiates energy from the miniature garbage can, taunting me.

My phone tells me it is 8:15 p.m. I'm late. Melanie has already texted asking where I am.

I text her: *Not feeling well suddenly. Homebound for the evening. I'll make it up to you. Sorry!*

Clenching my teeth, I reach in and snatch the crumpled flyer, unsnarling it from itself. I place it on the island in our closet, then enter the address into GPS on my cellphone.

He must be there. I think.

Staring at the flyer, more thoughts present themselves.

What if it's an actual open house?

What if he really is in Las Vegas?

What if he isn't there, but people he knows see you?

What if it's nothing?

You don't know what you're walking into.

"I don't care," I say out loud, and mean it. It's true, I don't care anymore. I need to know more than I need anything else. I can't stay in this purgatory.

My headlights become prominent on the road in front of me as the sunlight hides behind the horizon. My nerves dance at the unknown of what I will find in the shadows of the night.

I'm driving to an unknown house alone, at night, because of a flyer I found in a stupid little garbage can. "This is ridiculous," I say aloud, shaking my head, but I keep driving.

My phone dings, alerting me to a text message. I tap at my phone resting in its cradle to unlock it. Gliding through the commands, I open the text message.

Ben: Call me. It's important. Or you can stop by. #145

Just as I finish reading the text, my phone sings a loud ring through my car's speakers, and my muscles tighten in a quick jolt. My finger races to mute the noise with a press of a button on my steering wheel.

"Hello? Soph, it's me." Ben's deep voice fills my car like a dense cloud of smoke.

I stay silent.

"Soph? Are you there? Oh god, please." His voice cracks with panic.

"I'm here," I assure him.

"Sophia, please. You must believe me, I'm so sorry." His strong, deep voice fights through frantic worry.

"Ben, it wasn't okay—but I know you wouldn't hurt me."

The air cracks as he rustles with his phone. "You know I love you, right? I know I never said *those* words, but I was, and am, still madly in love with you." He pauses, and my car goes silent. "The only joy I have is thoughts of you; I think about being tangled with you in the dark after we make love and laughing together, feeling content knowing that your genuine laugh is because of me, and in that moment, you're mine." There's a long pause. My heart becomes packed tightly with agony.

"Ben?"

"Yeah, I'm here." His tears are no longer hidden by his deep voice as it breaks with each word. "Sophia, I always loved you." He inhales sharply, the tears stealing his breath. "Everything I've ever done since meeting you was for you. You're always on my mind. You must know that I'm sorry." The phone crackles some more.

"Ben? You're scaring me."

Silence.

"Ben?" I push, my mind buzzing with worry.

"Anything you might hear…fuck, I'm sorry." His deep voice is gone, replaced by solid sobs.

"Ben, please tell me what's wrong. What happened? Talk to me."

He sucks in a deep breath, gaining strength to speak. "They'll be coming for me soon. I just want you to know everything I've ever said, I meant. You've made my life better and my heart happy. I can't picture my world without you in it."

"Ben, what does that mean?" My heart cracks right down the middle. His desperate voice crushing me. The worry in his voice infectious.

"I'll be waiting for you there, alone." His voice fractures completely with his final words that mean more than just "I love you." He ends the call as music again spills from my speakers, replacing his deep, wounded voice.

14

Newbie

My mind races with concern over Ben's phone call, my fingers tingling from a slight adrenaline release. While Ben is known for dramatics to get my attention, the sheer panic in his voice shook me. He wasn't putting it on for attention. He was genuinely scared. I reach to call him back, but my throat becomes increasingly dry when my phone instructs me to take the next exit. I force what spit I can manage down in one big swallow, allowing the disturbing phone call to take a backseat in my sea of anxiety.

My body flushes with heat, creating a muggy discomfort. I adjust my thermostat from the controls on my steering wheel to blast me with cool air. I also crack the window, flooding the crisp autumn evening air into my car. It dances around my skin, kissing the back of my damp neck.

My stomach vibrates as if processing a meal I will regret

eating. I've always had a nervous stomach; something both Cassidy and I share. I grip my leather steering wheel, rolling it to the right, taking the exit.

I find myself in a decrepit neighborhood that was probably spectacular in the 1970s. Rolling through a stop sign, I see many cars ahead parked on both sides of the battered, curbless asphalt road. All the cars are nice, new, expensive. None belong in this neighborhood. A brand-new silver Audi A7 catches my eye, causing my heart to stop.

"Rob?" I mutter, but exhale remembering his is at home, parked in our garage.

Slowly driving past the split-level house displayed on the flyer, my GPS announces that I've arrived. I stop slightly past it and peer through my back passenger window. I compare it to the house on the flyer, confirming it's the same. A single exterior porch light kisses the dark front porch with vague yellow light, while another tall pathway light incased in yellow glass offers direction through the shadows. The black windows give the appearance that the home is empty.

The home is surrounded by tall, aged trees, giving little privacy from the surrounding houses that are situated only yards away. The homes on each side of the open house are occupied. Numerous cars of varying decay occupying the driveway of the left one, and tacky lawn ornaments occupying the front yard of the right. Each lit from within, but cheap battered blinds are drawn on both.

"What? I don't get it." I question myself for coming here.

I whip around in my seat, examining the many cars parked up and down the street. The owners of these cars must be somewhere.

"Screw it," I say with a frustrated exhale, then quickly turn my car around in a neighbor's driveway. I pull over, parking behind a new, slick black Mercedes E300.

Gripping my steering wheel so tightly my knuckles whiten, I peer out my window. I don't see any movement through the black windows of the house. Shutting my car off, I swiftly check myself in the rearview mirror. I tuck my Gucci Marmont Matelassé crossbody bag under my seat, then cram the flyer into my coat pocket and my keys in the other. If I need to run, I'll only need my keys.

I step out of my car into the chilly night, making sure to shut the door quietly. Muffled bass breaks the unbending silence. My senses search for the source by quickly studying all cars; it might be someone in a car listening to music, but I discover the faint bass is coming from the open house. It's almost undetectable, but my vibrating nerves would allow me to hear a whisper.

My black leather heels click on the dry pavement until I reach the driveway, where I begin crunching dry pine needles with each step. I stroll to the front door with the dim yellow light, passing a car in the driveway that looks like one of Rob's acquaintance's, Jacob Hope. As a matter of fact, I'm positive it's Jacob's car. He's a strange man who is always a big donor at my charity events. He's always polite to me, but he seems too uptight to be out this late.

At the door, the dim yellow porch light illuminates a noticeable mark on the house directly under it. The mark appears to be the symbol on the flyer carved into the siding of the house.

I knock.

No answer.

I knock again.

I wait.

Still no answer.

I knock again.

The door cracks open and a petite woman peers through the small opening, looking me up and down. Her beautiful foxlike face displays narrow and pointy features, and her flawlessly applied makeup accentuates them.

"Flyer?" her airy voice demands.

I fumble, trying to pull out the crumpled flyer I stuffed in my pocket. I unravel it and hand it to her with two hands. Her facial expression gives her away; she didn't expect me to produce it. She looks me up and down again.

"Okay," she states as an answer to an unasked question, and opens the door. "I'm Ana," she says sternly as I slip through the door she cracks just enough for my body.

Her tight leather pants and short black top accentuate her thin frame. Her straight golden blond hair cut in a sharp bob above her shoulders bounces easily with her focused movements. Her skeletal feet are bare and display freshly painted red toenails.

The door closes quickly behind me. Her delicate fingers lock the two deadbolts, as well as the doorknob lock.

I nervously turn away from the door to see what I'm being locked into. Heavy black plastic sheeting hangs from the ceiling, allowing only room for three bodies at the door. Artificial yellow light bleeds through a crack in the plastic sheeting. The bass now pulses persistently at my feet, but it's still incredibly muffled.

"Phone stays here." She points at a large glass dish taking up all the space on a small entry way table. The dish overflows with cellphones.

"I didn't...I don't have mine," I announce as my right hand clutches my mother's cross hanging at my chest.

"I'll check?" she says, sounding like both a question and a statement.

I nod.

She pats me down and is content.

"This way," her breathy voice declares over her lanky shoulder, holding open the black plastic sheeting for me to walk through. "Here," she hands me an oversized, but delicate black lace mask, "put it on, please."

With my trembling hands, I manage to put the mask on my face as we walk up the narrow, thickly carpeted stairs. The felt-covered black mask adorned with lace trim covers most of my face above my nose, leaving the tip of my nose and eyes uncovered.

Reaching the top of the stairs, she turns to me, her face now masked, too, and asks if I would like a beverage before my introduction. I say no. She smiles as she reaches for me, gripping my hand, leading me into an empty, tiny kitchen with dim yellow overhead lighting from the low ceiling. Even if Rob were here, it would be hard to make him out quickly in this lack of light.

A massive silky black dog stands tall, perching in the corner of the tiny kitchen with its eyes intently on me. Its ears pointing straight up as Ana says in an impressively assertive voice for her size, "Sit, Babe." The dog's gigantic head shifts from me to Ana, then the dog follows the command. His gargantuan head stays pointed at Ana, but his eyes shift between us.

"Here, party favor." She hands me a double shot of something dark and a round orange pill with an imprint of Buddha on it.

"No, really, I…" She pushes the shot glass to my lips and I allow her, tilting my head back to assist.

"Good girl. Another?" she asks. The gemstones on her mask shimmer in the vague lighting.

I shake my head, but she ignores my answer again, pouring more alcohol, offering another double shot. I tilt my head back again, swallowing the dark liquid, then try not to choke as it sets my throat on fire.

She watches me intently. Her eyes flash between my face and my hand holding the round orange pill. I slowly raise my hand holding the pill, opening my palm to show it. She offers me a nod with an assuring smile. I pinch the pill between the thumb and index finger of my other hand then place the pill on my tongue, Buddha side up.

"There, all better. Now come." She reaches for my hand but doesn't grab it as before. Instead, she waits for me to reach for hers, and I do. She holds my hand until we reach the second floor landing, where she releases me and gracefully swings her hips with each step down in front of me.

I reach into my mouth for the pill, but it is mostly dissolved. I flick the remaining portion onto the carpeted floor at the base of the narrow, dark stairs as she opens an old hollow door made of thin wood.

On the other side of the door, a poorly lit hallway offers two directions: left or right. A muscular mask-free man standing against the wall with his arms folded scans me with his eyes, his head motionless.

She continues to the right and slides into the first door on the left, closing it behind us.

"Normally, this is where you would change because street clothes are not allowed. However, since you're new, you're allowed one introduction in your clothing. I do need your shoes, coat, and car keys, though."

I stare at her, confusion causing my brows to droop. She cocks her head to the left and raises her brows. I follow her simple directions by sliding my coat off my shoulders, leaving my keys in the pocket. She extends her hand for the coat, and I lean to hand it to her. I then bend over to slip my heels off one by one.

She places my coat in a locker tucked in the corner of the tiny room full of lockers, then hands me a key with the number 21 engraved on it.

"You can put your shoes in there, too."

I again follow directions and place my shoes in the locker. I close it and lock it, then place the key around my wrist with the red elastic coil it hangs from.

I want to ask her where I am. What "introduction" is she talking about? Is Rob here? Does she know him? Why the black plastic sheeting over all the windows and entrance? What was that pill? Where is everyone? But I'm worried these questions would prove I don't belong here, and she'd have the guy in the hallway kick me out. I don't know the rules of this place. I wasn't invited to this open house; it was my husband who was invited.

"Hair down, honey."

I take my hair out from my high ponytail and let it fall around my face.

She examines me and says, "Desperate housewife. They'll love that," and giggles. Her face tight from her smile surprises me; her sharp, foxlike features bend into an innocent brightness, changing her allure completely.

She slips out the door hurriedly, expecting me to follow her, and begins spitting rules at me over her shoulder. She walks speedily down the hallway towards the bass, passing the muscular man again with his arms still folded. Her hips sway side-to-side with ease, but my feet struggle to keep up in the dark unfamiliar territory. I only hear a few rules like, "No means no," "Honor rules set with your partner," and, "Maintain all activities here." We pass a few dark rooms that have no doors, each decorated with faint red lights and occupied with naked men and women. I frantically search for Rob as we scurry past each doorframe. She stops at yet another door at the end of the long hallway. The door brandishing the symbol from the flyer. The ominous metal door doesn't appear to belong in this house.

"And, obviously, privacy is imperative." She says the final rule as she faces me and scans me intently, then offers another youthful smile. She opens the large door behind her with twist of the large stainless-steel doorknob and a bump of her leather-covered behind.

15

Veronica

"Enjoy your evening," my hostess says upon my entering the room. I turn to her for direction, but the door closes, trapping me in the loud mysterious room.

I open my mouth to object to her leaving me, but a flash of courage stops me. Sucking in my breath, my hands balled at my side, I swivel on my heels towards the loud, crowded room.

The music's thunderous bass rattles in my chest, competing for space within my ribcage. I immediately scan the room for Rob. The room's cool air nips at my damp skin.

I don't see his face, but I instantly notice the room doesn't belong in this house. This entire portion of the basement has been remodeled into a modern, elegant one-room club. The red rope lighting tucked under the chic coffered ceiling offers just enough light to see throughout the large room. There are tall leather booths along the wall closest to me, and a bar in the furthest corner, complete with glass shelving crowded with various liquor bottles. Behind the bar, a husky shirtless man in a leather mask covering his entire head deals drinks. The room is full of people in various masks.

Some notice my entrance, turning in unison to stare. My body twinges with discomfort. I want to leave, but my desire to know more calms the instinct to escape. I stand in place, careful not to make eye contact as I nervously spin my wedding ring with the tip of my thumb. Thoughts of Rob flood my mind, further prompting my desire to know more about this place.

I walk towards the bar through a small crowd with my head down. Once there, I push a lit scented candle out of my way and stand on the tips of my toes, leaning forward to catch the bartender's attention. I ask what's available and get another full shot glass shoved at me by the bartender. The scented candle's powerful aroma mixes with the smell of sweet sweat that swirls through the room. I take the shot, trying not to pucker my face as the bitter taste disperses through my mouth. The hardness of the eyes watching me seems to ease as the alcohol warms my belly, then begins to slowly pulsate through my veins, mixing with the existing booze.

A figure enters my space and the smell of zesty citrus cologne sails into my nostrils, followed by warm breath on my ear.

"Sophia, we aren't supposed to use names here, but I must say I am surprised," a man's smooth, deep voice says clearly in my ear through the music that forces him to raise his voice to be heard.

I turn, finding a smile of straight, bright white teeth, a

chiseled jawbone, and a bare chest. It's Jacob Hope. That *was* his car in the driveway.

I smile blushingly. I don't know what to say. I don't know what's the wrong or right thing to say. I don't even know where I am.

"A fortunate room to have you in it," Jacob says, his full lips almost touching my ear. He moves away slightly to show me his killer smile again. His black beltless dress pants rest on his hips, allowing all six abdomen muscles to be seen in the dim red light. His green eyes narrow on me as he runs the knuckles of his left hand briefly down my arm, prompting my eyes to meet his. He peers down at me with fascination.

His black mask and suntanned skin distinct against his light blonde hair and glistening green eyes cause me to peer back at him with curiosity.

A woman approaches the bar behind Jacob and begins speaking to the bartender. I can't hear her words through the music, but her lips move in a distinctive, puckered way and I recognize her mouth; I'd recognize that teeth to gum ratio anywhere. It's Amy Baker, a well-known businesswoman in Deep River. She's on the board of a charity I do fundraisers for. I turn guiltily, positioning my body so that my half-masked face cannot be seen by her.

Amy's clothes, or lack thereof, make me blush for her until my mind settles on the normalcy of her attire in this setting. Her thick thighs bare, vibrating with each step away from the bar. Her nipples only covered by tiny red rectangles attached to strings that wrap endlessly around her neck and ribs. Her bottom bare, with a red string hiding between each bulky cheek. She stops at a tall round table, setting down the three drinks she was carrying, being happily greeted by the men who waited for her. A strobe light near her table flashes intensely, making each of her movements skip a beat. Each man at her table is in a mask, while exhibiting various forms of nakedness. The most dressed man, wearing only unbuttoned jeans that hug his curved ass, greets her by gripping one bulky ass cheek before taking her mouth into his own. Each of their movements is slowed by the strobe light, intensifying my confusion caused by the booze and pill mixture.

I look away shyly, but my shyness erodes as the music, the lights, the booze, and that pill mix into a collective hypnotic grace. The energy here soothes me. My agitation is distracted by it, forcing it into submission.

I scan the room again, noticing two mostly naked blonde women kissing, touching each other, while a small group of men and women watch. A woman sitting on a man's lap strokes him between her legs as they watch the women together. I shift my eyes away, only to see a naked man bent over a half-naked woman on a leather booth along the wall, forcing wails of pleasure from her that are lost in the booming music. Each powerful thrust forces her forward, but his hard grip on her hips keeps her in place.

"Don't be nervous," Jacob says, standing behind me, gently gripping both my arms and speaking into my ear. The unknown stops me again from asking if Rob is here. I'm not sure if Jacob assumes that Rob knows I'm here.

Jacob's bare feet position themselves behind me now, as he lightly caresses my arms with his fingertips. My skin tingles with raised bumps from his touch as I continue to scan the room. No one is fully dressed. Everyone is naked or in some form of lingerie like Amy's. Various couplings throughout the room. Various sexual acts.

I don't see Rob.

Jacob pushes his chin against my ear, forcing my head to tilt to the side, "Normally, Rob would have to be here with you, but for you, an exception is welcomed."

Jacob confirms it, Rob isn't here.

I close my eyes tightly, leaning back into him, allowing the alcohol to quiver through my body, making my legs heavy, followed by an unfamiliar rush of elation.

An unknown man speaks to Jacob as I continue to lean against his chest. I hazily hear their voices through the music but not their words. The man walks in front of me. His muscles protrude from under his brown skin and his length rests limp on his firm thigh. His thick brown hair naturally curls, creating perfect ringlets that fall down his masked forehead. He grips each of my wrists, pulling me to him until our foreheads gently collide. Our bodies sway to the music and I close my eyes, relinquishing control to the intensity of ecstasy cascading over my fear, coating it like cough syrup down a sore throat. The relief encouraging me to relax into it.

From behind, pushing my head to the side again, Jacob touches his lips to the base of my neck, and I reach back with one hand, gently fisting his thick blonde hair. My skin shudders with raised bumps again as his lips continue down my neck.

My mind is free from all the dark thoughts that have forcibly taken over my life as the elation intensifies, and my body becomes rootless.

Jacob slides down one strap of my dress together with one bra strap while delicately kissing the now bare skin. I watch a couple pleasuring each other on another leather booth over the unknown naked man's shoulder, his length now hard as it presses against me. A throbbing between my thighs begins deep from within my core. Its appetite scorching through my limbs.

My tranquility releases in waves. The hate that had enveloped me dissipates. The room is filled with people who don't care about the rioting in the streets, the murders of women in their city, or their broken hearts. For the first time in years, I'm at peace. Each touch of my skin tingles up my spine. Is this what Rob does this for? This feeling? Is this why he hurts me?

Jacob speaks to me, but I don't hear his words; they are lost in the ocean of music and pleasure. With each word, I feel his long blonde eyelashes tickle my cheek. I inhale his intoxicating zesty cologne as he unzips my dress, sliding it down to the floor, creating a pool of red viscose around my feet with my locker key resting on top of it.

I don't feel exposed. I don't feel scared. For the first time, I feel as if I'm exactly where I belong.

The naked man in front of me kisses my lips lightly, gripping the skin of my outer thigh forcefully, while Jacob caresses my shoulders and kisses my neck. Each kiss building the aching anticipation between my thighs. I close my eyes, now fully surrendering to the feverish elation.

What if Rob were to walk in right now? The thought graces my intoxicated mind and makes me want more. I want Rob to see me.

The naked muscular man stops kissing me and curiosity triggers my eyes to flutter open. The man is talking to an unfamiliar woman in a black lace mask similar to mine. Her black lace panties and bra are like mine except she is wearing black thigh-high hose complete with a black lace garter belt. Her hair is the same color as mine, and even the same length. I am looking at a sexier, more daring version of myself. I hear him confirm "two thousand," and she nods her head, giving a splendid smile.

He steps away.

Jacob stays, delicately running his lips along the nape of my neck.

Her exquisite lips tighten around her teeth in a playful smile as she steps closer, now standing in the space the unknown naked man possessed.

I welcome the softness of the back of her hand against my face. Leaning into her caress, I close my eyes to feel her touch fully. Using her hand to lift my chin, she kisses me. Her silky kiss causes pressure to grow at the base of my spine. My hips wiggle as my thighs tighten, squeezing my pulsing core.

My knees weaken, completely drunk from her kiss. I lean back into Jacob's bare chest as he slides his rough hand up my back, gripping my bra clasp. He pulls on the clasp in one quick, effortless movement. As it falls, joining my dress on the floor, a rush of cold air encloses my tightened nipples.

Every touch on my skin is magnified. Each touch causes an extravagant tingling sensation, instigating my body to plead for another, begging for a release from the pressure now growing unbearable between my thighs.

She leans over my shoulder, "I want her," she says to Jacob.

"No, Veronica. Share," he replies sternly through the loudness of the room. His nose nudges the side of my head as he takes my earlobe into his mouth.

She nods slowly, signaling her agreement to his proposition.

She kisses me incompletely, pulling away to stare at me with her mahogany eyes. Gripping my hand, she leads me out of the room, with Jacob following, leaving my clothes and locker key on the floor of the loud and crowded room.

We walk together, the three of us kissing, stroking, petting. We sloppily make our way down the hallway I entered from, then into one of the rooms I passed earlier filled with dim red light.

16

Savior's Softness

My doorbell hums. The irritating noise assaults my throbbing head. Cracking one eye open, I fight through blurriness to read the time on my phone. The bright display shows 9:05 a.m. My mouth's dryness makes it painful to open.

The doorbell hums again. My eyes burn each time I attempt to open them.

The previous night surges into my mind, followed by a prickly realization that I'm hungover. I sit up and my head throbs, threatening to explode as my eyes flood with white specks. My mind refuses to focus through the hangover, but there's also a hint of another aching I'm unfamiliar with. My sluggishness makes me suspect its residue from the pill I was given.

I stand, placing my hand against the wall to find balance and gain clear eyesight free of white specks. The irritating noise of the doorbell continues. I notice I'm wearing my red viscose dress that Jacob had removed the night before. I pass a full-length mirror as I exit my bedroom and see smudged mascara under my eyes. I lick my fingertips to rub it away, but it won't budge.

The doorbell hums again. With each step I take, I'm reminded of the sex I had last night that has left me raw. I touch my face with embarrassment while the memories from last night continue to float into my mind without permission.

Peeking through the textured glass making up most of the real estate on my entryway door, I see Detectives Cruz and Valletta.

I hesitate.

The doorbell hums again. I reach for the door, opening it so my body is positioned behind it. I'm squinty-eyed and still sleepy—possibly still drunk.

"Detectives?" My voice fights through my painfully dry throat.

"Mrs. Claire. May we have a moment of your time?" she asks, completely ignoring my appearance, but Valletta gawks at the mess of a woman before him.

"Yes." I open the door wider for them to enter. "Will you give me a minute?"

"Of course, we'll be right over there." She points to the couch she sat on before.

I waddle back to my bedroom and quickly strip off my clothes, wash my face, and brush my teeth. I chug a bottle of water while I pee. I put on my robe knowing I need to shower once they leave. I hurry back to my sitting room where the detectives wait.

"I'm sorry," I apologize for taking so long upon entering the room, even though I'm not entirely sure how long I've been gone.

"I'm sorry to arrive unannounced, but we've received some news," she jumps right in.

I try to focus on this visit I half expected, but my mouth is still painfully dry.

I interrupt her. "Would you like anything to drink?" I ask politely as I rise to fetch myself more water. She declines. Valletta remains silent, his eyes concentrated on my movement.

I sit next to her with my full glass of water at my lips and she continues, "There was another murder. Two nights ago."

"I hadn't heard," I moan in between gulps.

A phone rings a generic tone. Cruz reaches into her grey suit pocket, handing the ringing cellphone to Valletta. He answers and begins to argue loudly in Spanish.

"Your husband," Cruz strains to speak over Valletta, but his voice overpowers hers. "Jesus Christ, Valletta!" Detective Cruz shouts over his booming voice. With a slight glare from him, followed by a nod towards the front door, Valletta marches outside to finish his heated conversation. As his long legs make the trek to my front door in a hurry, his tight white polo gives away a tattoo, text only, on his upper back.

She continues, "A man matching the description of your husband, as well as his car was last seen with three of the women. We knew Mr. Claire was romantically linked to each, but... Sophia, we arrested someone else. Someone who looks like your husband and drives a similar car. We arrested Benjamin

Booth."

My throat contracts and I choke on water, causing a violent coughing fit. My body convulses with each cough. I try to compose myself but my throat flexes insistently, forcing me to cough harder. She scoots closer to me, patting me on my back.

"You okay?" She pats more. I nod through a slightly less dramatic cough.

"What did you say?" I croak.

"The fentanyl citrate used in the murders has a special indicator in its manufactured compound, meaning it is unique to Anexa, specifically Trimble Laboratories. Sophia, do you know why Benjamin Booth was fired from Anexa?"

I attempt to speak but I choke on my words, patting my chest to help clear the water I inhaled.

"Sophia, we know about your history with Benjamin Booth. During questioning…he's been very forthcoming. I know he's the one…the affair you had mentioned at the deli. I believe you're in serious danger. He's completely fixated on you."

I laugh. Not just a small chuckle. But I actually laugh at her, as if she's told a hilarious joke. "He wouldn't hurt me," I say coldly.

"Sophia," she begins to plead.

"Adella," I reply kindly, hoping I didn't offend her by laughing at her. "Really, I'm the last person Benjamin Booth would ever hurt."

"Sophia," she smiles and removes her hand from my back, "I know you; I know the type. I've seen it and I know how this will end. It's heartbreaking and preventable," she bargains, sounding like an after-school special. "Remember that I said I lit a candle for my sister?"

I nod. I know the beautiful detective is attempting to sooth me. Attempting to create a bond of trust. But all I can focus on is her mouth and how it curves as she speaks.

She locks her eyes on me and continues, "My sister, she was in a situation like yours. She couldn't see past her love of a bad man. We lived with our father, who tried to stop her from leaving, from being with such a man. But she was old enough to leave, so she did. She moved in with him. For my father, it was like my mother leaving him all over again, but far worse; it was his daughter leaving his safety."

She clears her throat, fighting the discomfort from sharing this information, but continues, "She had disappeared." Her fingers fiddle with each other in her lap as she recalls more. "The bad man, her boyfriend, found her dumped on the wet grass of their front lawn." Cruz clears her throat again, adding, "I don't know if it was him who gave her the hot shot or someone wanting to get his attention. I was young, and he was murdered a few years later."

She glances down at the floor, then up at the ceiling and continues, "My father tried to find the answers we all wanted about her death but wasn't successful before a heart attack took his life. My grandmother claims his heart was broken too many times and couldn't handle the pain." She shakes her head in two fast jolts, shaking off the emotions that forced themselves into her by sharing the story of her sister. I want to say that I know. I want to explain that I researched her and know about her sister and her mother, but I wasn't aware of her father's death. My heart hurts for her.

Her dark eyes meet mine again. "My point is, we all have people who care about us. Our choices influence those people. It's up to us to make the right choices, if not for ourselves, then for them."

She places her hand on my robe-covered thigh and continues, "Benjamin Booth is dangerous. I know you can see it. Just try to see past your history with him." She leans in enough for me to smell her again. Her smooth, comforting scent draws me in.

There is a sense of security when I'm with her, and I'm thankful she is on my side. She is the only person I know who is untainted in my now unrecognizable life.

I glance down at her petite hand on my thigh and the world is muted, with only my heartbeat breaking the silence. This excitement is different. It's calm. I'm in control.

She stands abruptly.

My control is fleeting.

"Sophia." She pushes her shoulders back and corrects herself, "Mrs. Claire…" Cruz fumbles more with her words that end with something about being safe tomorrow. "You would be better off not opening the door for trick-or-treaters." She walks herself to the front door and barks for Valletta to start the car.

Locking my front door, I question my feelings towards the young detective. Am I wrong? Am I not reading her correctly?

I can't grasp the truth. Any normalcy seems miles away from my existence. My mind dulls with desire and caution. My concentration grasping for what is right and wrong—what is acceptable behavior. My moral compass cracking, with no will left to guide it. The edges of my reality have been singed.

Showering helps clear some of the ache from my body, but it's still sluggish and sore. I bring my laptop to bed with me, sitting in the darkened room with the bright display almost too intense for my still tender eyes.

I gulp more water before typing, letting it dribble down my chin before smearing it across my mouth with the back of my hand. How could they think it's Ben? That must have been what he was frantic about when he called.

I Google Ben.

My search results in many articles, as well as his LinkedIn, Facebook, and Deep River's Chamber of Commerce sites. I click on the first article with a headline that reads, "Trimble Laboratories Employee Terminated After Alleged Theft."

DEEP RIVER, Wa. — Anexa, a local research, development, and advanced technologies company with worldwide interests, has fired its director of policy for Trimble Laboratories after he was accused of theft.

The company says in a statement that Benjamin Booth had worked for the company for five years. Booth's firing comes after the company's longtime chief financial officer, Kevin Graham, accused Benjamin Booth of artificially inflating sales. However, it was the founder and chief executive officer of Anexa, Robert Charles Claire, who fired Benjamin Booth due to accusations of abuse of exclusive rights to intellectual property for personal incentive. The local and well-known CEO had little to say about the incident.

Sources close to both parties say Benjamin Booth had been fighting a personal battle with addiction. A battle that had been made very public after an accident in which he was under the influence and later charged with vehicular manslaughter.

Mr. Booth has denied all current accusations by Trimble Laboratory and Anexa. His attorneys are certain the charges against him will be dropped, as they claim there is a "considerable lack of evidence."

I knew Ben kept his secrets, but I had no idea about his addiction, or that it caused such harm to others.

Thinking about the drug that had been stolen from Trimble's lab on Anexa's campus and used to murder the women—only women my husband has slept with—creates a sticky knot in my throat. Gripping the ice-cold glass of water, I gulp until it's gone, which slightly loosens the knot. My head feels as if a thousand rubber bands are squeezing it, daring it to give in to the pressure.

I can see how Ben's ethics may be under question after Rob accused him of such a thing. It makes sense. Ben also has the same taste in women as Rob and has probably—unintentionally—shared one of the deceased in their bed. The two men even look and dress the same. It's remarkable, actually.

Detective Cruz invades my focus once again. I still can't be sure if my feelings towards her are honest. My thoughts muddy as I attempt to navigate right from wrong. The normalcy of daily life floats further away from me as my mind clouds with desire for more risk. A dull yearning for Ben to comfort me, to draw me back into reality, flows through my body before rushing to my head.

I reach for my now empty glass, desperately needing more water.

Padding down the hall to the kitchen, I focus on Ben. I know

Ben wasn't stealing from Trimble Labs, but then again, I didn't know he had a heinous addiction problem that killed someone. I pour ice-cold water into a taller glass, then grip three bottles of water before making my way back into my bedroom. My strength diluting with each step.

Ben hated Rob and made it clearer with each passing day while we were together, and even more so after I broke it off. If Rob had known about Ben and me, and that's why he fired him in such a way that destroyed Ben's career, Rob would make me pay for it, too. Dearly.

Ben would say incredibly hateful things about Rob, which I always attributed to simple jealousy. He would grow increasingly agitated as the time neared for me to leave his home to go back to my house with Rob. He would beg for me to stay, knowing that if I stayed, our secret would come out.

Ben isn't a murderer. My Ben wouldn't hurt anyone, except for maybe my husband. God, he hated Rob. He hated that I stayed regardless of the cheating and emotional abuse. He hated the way Rob treated both women and men. He hated Rob's smug arrogance. He hated how successful he was, even though Ben had worked much harder in life than Rob ever had. Most importantly, it set his soul on fire that I chose Rob, my husband, over him. Still, he couldn't kill, even to get back at Rob.

I'm a silly woman; I still miss the softness Ben only had towards me. There was something so endearing about watching him verbally assassinate someone then turning to me and smiling his loving and sexy smile.

I curl into the thick long pillow now tucked between my legs. I close my eyes and picture Ben's hard naked chest as I dance my fingers around the thick scar it brandishes. Running my hand down the peaks and valleys of his chest and abs as I draw in his scent. His scent a mix of light cologne and skin that had been warmed by the sun.

My eyes close as sleep takes me to a peaceful place. My last thought of Ben forces a small, satisfied smile. I picture looking up at him as my head still rests on his chest, his chin turns down towards me as he presses his lips to my forehead, holding them there as he squeezes me tightly in his arms.

17

Cassidy

I follow the dream again, eager to know the ending. My arms extended to my sides and my fingers spread wide with the harsh wind blowing around them. Wearing the cotton nightgown that hangs down to my ankles, I stand on the edge of the tall building with the wind violently whipping around me as Rob reaches desperately for me. His frightful serpent head gone, replaced by his handsome face displaying agonizing concern as his hands grasp for me. His mouth bends with his strong words as veins protrude from his neck with his frenzied effort, though his exertion in gaining my attention fails; his voice cannot penetrate the now deafening wind atop the tall city building.

I turn towards the edge again, reaching for my mother's cross necklace that hangs from my neck to find that it is no longer there. Looking down at the city streets, peace fills my heart watching the toy-sized cars drive the miniature streets. The violent wind is soothing, rocking me unpredictably from toes to heels on the ledge. The comfort of the potential fall envelopes me as I close my eyes, lifting my arms in the air like a baby bird. I exhale and release all the worry, hate, and sadness from my heart just as Rob grips my extended arm within his large hand, burning my skin with his tight grip. He rips my body from the edge of the building, tearing me away from the complete peace I had just seconds ago.

My eyes blink furiously at him as he stands between me and the ledge of the building. His handsome face still speaks to me with silent words that disappear into the loud wind. His mouth bending with each frantic word. I step to him, enthusiastic to embrace his tall body in my arms.

A sharp poke in my lower back rips my mind from standing in front of Rob on the building's roof. My back is poked again by a dull pointy tip bringing me fully out of the dream. I shift my body away from the assault, pushing through my hot jumbled sheets. Another determined poke presses at my back. My mind awakens rapidly, as I rise angrily to meet the poker. My eyes try to focus on the figure now standing at the foot of my bed.

She's smiles and giggles.

"Don't you know it's two, Soph?" she teases.

"Cassidy?" My voice rasps, thoroughly annoyed by my little sister.

I have a sharp memory of the day she rushed into my room in the apartment we shared, poking at me furiously. Her normally gentle voice shrieking nonsense as I tore my mind from deep sleep. I remember her pale face wet with tears as I cupped her face in my hands and asked her to calm down, to tell me what was wrong. That's when she told me that mom and dad were both dead. I regret more than anything in my life not being the one who answered the door when the police came to inform us. I wished Cassidy didn't live in my apartment. I wished I could have somehow braced her better for the loss of our parents.

"Hey, sis. I was in town and wanted to come say hi." Her voice is cheery and childlike. She plops onto my bed, sitting close, causing the bed to fall beneath me, and I'm forced to readjust.

"It's two o'clock?" I question the afternoon light dancing through the cracks of my curtains, trying to make sense of it.

"Yes, silly." She bounces on the bed where she sits.

"What day is it?" I ask, feeling the heat of my bedding around me and beads of sweat on my exposed skin being cooled by the ceiling fan.

"Day? What do you mean, *day*?" She nudges me playfully.

"Water, please?" I ask, genuinely needing water but also needing to compose myself. As soon as she walks out of the room, I assess myself. Cupping my eyes with my palms, I rub them roughly. My body feels human again, but my muscles remain weak.

I must have slept all day and night, which means Rob will be home tomorrow evening.

I reach for my mother's cross that the hospital gave me when I picked up her and dad's belongings while Cassidy waited in my car. The cross I haven't removed from my neck since that day, but I find only bare skin. I run my fingers through my hair, then wipe the sweat from the nape of my neck before Cassidy walks back into my bedroom, carrying a full glass of water.

"Filtered?" I ask, reaching pathetically for it.

"Yes, weirdo. I know you won't drink it otherwise."

I tilt my head back, open my throat, and gulp down the entire glass.

"You feeling okay?" She places the back of her scrawny hand on my forehead, pretending she would know what to do if I were running a fever.

I moan yes.

"Why are you still in bed, then?"

I stay silent. My eyes remain down at my blanket-covered legs.

"How about some coffee?"

I nod.

She grips my hands, then leans her body back, using her minuscule body weight to slowly pull me out of bed. I grab my robe that I draped over my bed and slowly slide each arm into it, nervous that any quick movement will bring back the pounding headache. I tie the waist tightly, then quickly pull up the neckline to hide the fact that our mother's necklace is missing. With her arm around my shoulder, we sway together down the hall and into kitchen. She begins to prep the coffee, making her way around my kitchen as if it's her own. She lived with us for two months before finding another boyfriend to move in with.

I watch her move, each movement so confident. Her jeans are torn at the knees and loose fitting, only holding onto her lanky frame with the help of a belt. Her glossy ash brown hair reaches her waist, following a second behind each movement she makes. She looks like a hippy; a style I would never try, but on her it fits beautifully.

"Here," she says with a wink, sliding over a plate with one piece of toast smothered with peanut butter and a cup of fresh coffee with hazelnut coffee creamer.

"Water," I demand after taking the first bite of my toast, struggling to chew the toasted bread and peanut butter with virtually no saliva. She hands me another cup filled to the top with filtered water.

The tall grandfather clock that stands looming in the hallway chimes 2:15 p.m. Its chiming echoes off the walls, piercing my ears and shaking my brain.

"Why do you keep that creepy, loud thing?" Cassidy jokes.

"It's been in his family for centuries. His mother insisted we have it," I answer, looking at it with spite.

"What's wrong?" She stares at me while I study my toast, contemplating taking another bite.

I ignore her and redirect. "Why are you here?"

"I told you. I was in the area…" I cut her off with a flick of my wrist that calls her a liar and dares her to continue the lie. She readjusts her stance, then glides her way to my piano in the nook off the kitchen.

I chug the last of my water, then carefully lift the coffee cup to my lips, sipping its warm, sweet goodness. She sits at the piano, gently lifts the fall board, then begins to quietly play Erik Satie's "Gymnopédies No. 1." Its notes carry childhood memories with them. I'd listened to her practice every Tuesday and Thursday after school with old Ms. Mueller, our piano teacher. Ms. Mueller was not only the pianist at our church, but she was also the organist. She smelled of musty earth and her lipstick was always on her teeth.

I was never a good piano player, but Cassidy always was. She was a natural. As a child, I'd love to watch her make invisible magic by pressing the keys.

Carrying my coffee cup, I sit on the larger of the two sitting room chairs and listen intently, curling my knees to my chest. I take another sip of my coffee, allowing it to gradually flow life back into me as I pull the neckline of my robe up to hide my naked décolleté.

She stops playing, then looks down at her hands resting in her lap. "Are you going to tell me what's wrong?" she asks, hunched over like a child who was just told her parents are getting a divorce—pouty and wounded.

"I don't know where to start," I confess.

"Anywhere. You're not okay, I can tell." She speaks like a child needing her mother to tell her that despite the shitty circumstances, mommy will prevail and everything will be okay.

The honesty she is asking of me cannot be given. I cannot tell my baby sister about Rob's women, the strange man at the football game, the open house and Rob's secret parties, losing mom's necklace, or even worse, that the police think my lover is a murderer. It's my job to care for her since our parents' car accident—to protect her from the evils of the world.

I take a deep breath and exhale gradually. With grace, I look my sister in the eyes and lie. "Cass, I'm fine. I promise. Things are just tense right now. Rob is stressed with work and

I'm overloaded, too."

"When is he not stressed with work?"

"I know, but it's a large company. You must remember that he doesn't have a normal job. He never turns off. He can't walk out the door and be done for the day, knowing a paycheck will be delivered as promised. Rob has a department at his company just for paychecks. Do you see how heavy that burden would be?" I try explaining like I would to a child, then realize I'm defending Rob yet again.

Cassidy rolls her eyes. Having seen his temper on more than one occasion, her compassion for Rob has dwindled over the years.

"Cassidy, I'm fine. Really. I've been through worse," I say with a warm smile.

Cassidy returns the smile, showing that she is content, believing that I'm okay. And that, somehow, she has helped.

With her head now resting on my lap, her body curls into a tight ball at my feet. She clears her throat. "Soph?" Her voice floods the silence of the room.

"Mm?"

"Brooke Sadler and I were friends. You know, the employee of Anexa who was murdered?

"Oh, I didn't realize you were friends," I say, stroking her silky hair.

"Yeah, I actually got her the interview through Rob. She worked in his office for his chief financial officer as his assistant. She told me she was dating a man who was going to leave his wife for her. Should I tell the police? Maybe this boyfriend had something to do with her murder."

The need to defend Rob returns. "I doubt her boyfriend has killed all these women. Plus, the police are doing their job. I'm sure they know she was dating someone." The image of Rob holding Brooke by her throat against the wall of his office taunts me.

She glances up at me and nods in agreement. I offer her a wink.

"Remember when Angelo put me in the hospital?"

"Yes," I answer. The memory of her bruised and broken face skates into my mind. Her battered face is a memory the fuzziness of time hasn't been able to dull.

"When he had his belt around my throat, I could literally feel my body's energy slow to nothing. It was so scary," her voice cracks, "and I wonder if Brooke felt how I did. Did she also feel her breath slip from her?" She swallows the tears threatening to break her voice and continues, "It was such a terrible feeling, Soph." Her voice finally gives in to the tears as she rests her head back in my lap.

Still stroking her hair, I calm her. "Shhh, I don't think she was aware, honey. I think she just fell asleep, peacefully." I had this same conversation with her about our parents. She had nightmares for months after, envisioning the fear and pain our parents endured when the drunk driver hit them.

Cassidy looks up again with wide eyes, now dripping with tears. "I love you, Soph."

"I love you, too, Cass."

We sit in silence for a moment as I continue stroking her hair. I begin to hum "Too Ra Loo Ra Loo Ral" like our mother would when tucking us into bed as little girls.

Too ra loo ra loo ral
Too ra loo ra li
Too ra loo ra loo ral
That's an Irish lullaby

Mom's voice was so soft, sweet, and angelic when she sang those words. The warm thought of how different my life would be if she was still here engulfs my heart.

As I sit with Cassidy's head in my lap, I envision Brooke sashaying through Rob's main office, where his CFO's office is. Jealousy washes over me when I think of them beginning their affair with stares longer than normal, casual but accidental touches, then, eventually, making reasons to spend time together at the office before starting their affair outside the office. My body tenses knowing Rob probably hired her expecting to fuck her.

I begin to agonize over Rob not telling me at first that she was an employee, let alone that he knew her. Not only were they sleeping together, he worked closely with her daily.

We sit for a moment longer before Cassidy stands and stretches her long, skinny body, using her sleeve to wipe the wetness from her face.

"Well, I'm meeting some friends for dinner, so."

I stand to meet her, and we hug tightly. I wait to feel her release me before I let go. I collect my now empty coffee cup and walk to the kitchen with her following closely.

Setting my empty cup in the sink, she begins the routine I've been waiting for.

"Hey, Soph? I have…well, there's this cool company where I can sell stuff that really helps people. It's called LifeScent and I could be a Pod Leader and help others sell, too. I'd get really cool incentives and maybe even earn a vacation if I have enough sales."

I nod. "Okay," I say, waiting for the pitch to continue.

She gets bouncy with excitement explaining the latest multilevel marketing craze she wants to join. "I just need five hundred and fifty dollars to become a Trend Leader. I need to do it, like, now. So I can get in early. I just don't have that kind of money right now."

"So, you need to borrow five hundred and fifty dollars is what you're saying?"

She nods sheepishly and adds, "Also your Catwoman Halloween costume. There's a party I want to go to tonight, and it'll be purrfect," she purrs with a hint of smile.

"Are you sure it will fit?" I ask, eyeing Cassidy's behind playfully. "Let me grab my checkbook, and you know where my closet is."

She squeals with joy and kisses my face repeatedly.

I love this person—my sister. She is and always has been like a child of my own. It's best I protect her from my truths. She wouldn't know how to handle the information, anyway.

There are ways of doing things. Ways of getting what you want out of a bad situation. And the truth sometimes isn't it.

I smile as I write the check, knowing it will piss Rob off.

After handing her the check, she thanks me a few more times before we walk to her car. I notice a sticker of her last boyfriend's favorite rock band on the rear window. Cassidy was always notorious for mimicking her at-the-moment boyfriend's likes and dislikes, and they changed as quickly as the boyfriend.

I really had no idea she was friends with Brooke, which makes me a little nervous about how close she is to this mess.

18

Full Disclosure

I'm sitting at my dining table, slamming the keys of my laptop as I write a heated email to my event organizer who somehow has forgotten to confirm the musical guest. The creamy fabric of my pearl-colored cashmere sweater slides effortlessly over my skin, allowing my wrists the freedom to move with haste. I send the email, then open another regarding the event which states that the white linen napkins arrived, but they're teal. With a loud huff, I slam my laptop shut. I can manage this, but my ability to tolerate these mistakes is dwindling.

Another overcast day brings the occasional outpouring of sun through slits in the clouds. There's something about the dark, short days of the colder months that suggest shadowy possibilities which are easily ignored in the false security of sunlight.

Strolling to my front door to collect a package I heard

delivered moments ago, I open my door to see it waiting for me on the doorstep. The tiny white box is slightly crushed and decorated with various black scuff marks. I lock my door and set the alarm before entering Rob's office where I set the box down. Opening his desk to find his monogrammed letter opener, I use it to cut the tape along the flaps. I open the small box, then tear through the product packaging, removing the one levonorgestrel tablet from its sleeve. The large, round white pill sits in my open palm as I read the directions and warnings of, among other things, nausea.

I'm able to walk without being reminded of my night at the open house. A sense of guilt floods my mind occasionally, leaving me motionless as I question everything and everyone. I wonder what else in my life is going to reveal itself in this bizarre version of what I thought was my reality.

While I'm unable to have a baby with Rob, I'm still capable of becoming pregnant. This morning-after pill will ensure my night immersed in Rob's playground won't have any irreversible consequences.

I pour myself a glass of water in the kitchen, place the pill on my tongue, then gulp the entire glass. Placing my cup in the sink, I pause as I ponder how I'll dispose of the packaging so that Rob won't find it. I place the product packaging back into the scuffed box, then fold it closed. I could simply toss the box in the garbage; it's not as if he'll see it. But I can't chance it. I again wonder how Rob lives a life riddled with puzzles like this one with such ease. I decide to place the box in my car, a place he never goes, until I'm able to dispose of it elsewhere.

Standing at the towering windows that look out on Deep

River, a soupy mixture of confusion and discontentment swirls in my mind. I had expected a feeling of triumph after enfolding myself in Rob's secret life. I thought that once I sank my teeth into his world, I'd gain something. What, I'm not sure. Maybe the piece of me I slowly lost when I became Mrs. Claire.

I allow my mind to wander far from me, relaxing in the short pause where no thoughts exist. I watch the cars rush along the curves of the highway lanes, each lane its own separate vein in a much larger beast.

My doorbell hums, tearing me from my peaceful trance. I haven't had a visitor that hasn't in some way added to the anxiety that is slowly crushing me, crippling my ability to maintain even the simplest of responsibilities. I lean my head to the side, feeling a vertebra slide into place with a satisfying crack. I sweep any wrinkles from my black midi silk skirt and walk towards the door. As I grow closer, a faint ripple of amusement jolts through me as I see who is standing on the other side of the stained glass.

I disarm my alarm, slide the deadbolt, and open the heavy door. Leaning against the doorframe with crossed arms, I say nothing, but give a hint of a smile.

"Mrs. Claire."

"You're alone," I state the obvious, teasing my disbelief.

Detective Cruz shrugs her shoulders. "We don't always work together. This is my case." Her tone gives little away.

"What can I do for you?"

"We've had some recent revelations regarding Benjamin Booth that I'd like to discuss with you."

"Do you ever call?" I ask playfully.

She gawks at me and I can see her wheels turning. While anticipating her response, I'm unsure which person is standing before me: Adella or Detective Cruz.

I step back, swinging the large door wide open, giving her space to enter. "Please," I say with a gesture that invites her in. She steps just inside the door and respectfully waits. Her scent floats through the air, sending a delicious electric spark that starts in my abdomen, dances down my legs, and tingles my toes. I shut the door, locking the deadbolt.

"This way." I head towards the dining area, and Cruz follows closely.

"Please, sit," I say, motioning to the chair I pulled out for her. She does and unbuttons her grey jacket. I sit next to her at the head of the table, then cross my legs, allowing the cool silk fabric of my skirt to remain just a little too high.

"Water?" I offer.

"No, thank you," she declines. "Mrs. Claire…"

"Really, please, I'd like for you to call me Sophia," I request, using the sweetest voice I'm capable of. Not only do I want to remove the impersonal barrier between us, but I want her to see me as myself, not Rob's property.

"Sophia," she corrects herself, adding the slightest nod.

"So, what are these new revelations?" I ask with a warm smile.

"Well, Benjamin Booth claims you know more than you're sharing." She pauses, watching my response.

"I don't understand. Did you release him?"

"No, he's still in our custody. He's refusing to give DNA or answer further questions. His attorney claims they have already answered a plethora of unnecessary questions and refuse to answer more."

"He's not guilty. Not of this," I say, raising my brows and pursing my lips.

"Sophia, Benjamin's history may make you believe differently."

"What exactly are you referring to? The car accident or his addiction issues?" I ask, implying Ben had told me himself. My ego not allowing someone to know more than me about my Ben.

"It's not for me to divulge, but I can share some information that is connected to you," she says. "I think he's trying to shift culpability to you."

"Excuse me? Like he's saying I've killed people?" My eyes widen in shock. "He actually said that?" My voice becomes shrill.

"Well, no. If he did, this visit would be a very different one. He's simply offered open-ended suggestions."

"Suggestions? What do you mean? What did he suggest, exactly?" I spit at her, eager to know what Ben has said about me.

"Well, he suggested we look into your knowledge of Robert's affairs. Asked if you had motivations that may have been overlooked by myself and my team," she answers calmly, ignoring my anger.

I'm livid. A heat wave washes over me as this information settles in my mind. I am defending that little weasel while he's busy shifting blame anywhere he can. My upper lip curls with disgust.

The tall grandfather clock chimes from the hallway, echoing throughout the house. Its noise triggers a mild, dull ache behind my eyes. With my elbows on the table, I place my fingertips on my temples, pressing gently and massaging in circles.

"It's getting increasingly difficult to not think the worst when the worst keeps coming, just waiting outside my door," I say with my eyes closed as I continue massaging my temples.

"Hey," she whispers. I open my eyes to see Cruz gazing at me thoughtfully. "We know it wasn't you. Like I said, if there was any evidence, this would be a very different conversation."

"I know. I'm not worried about that." My throat betrays me, a raspy voice threatens tears. How do I explain that with Ben it was as if my soul had found something it left in another lifetime? An irresistible urge to cry washes over me as I mourn the death of the man I thought Ben was. Tears spill from my eyes.

"Hey, hey, hey," Cruz says as she leans forward. "I know. Benjamin has explained your relationship in detail. I know hearing what he has implied must hurt."

"He's an asshole," I say as tears continue to fall. The one person who I thought loved me turns out to be another fraud. Just like Rob.

"I'm sorry," she offers sweetly, then the corner of her bottom lip disappears into her mouth.

I lift my head, push my shoulders back, then reach for the tissue box sitting on the nearby credenza. "I'm fine, really. I shouldn't be surprised." I shrug and dab a tissue at my nose. "Ben and Rob are so similar." I let out a small, scornful chuckle.

"Yes, they are. While conducting interviews for this

investigation, some women wouldn't talk at all. Some would only answer questions about Benjamin. We believe Robert has some sort of agreement with some of the women."

"An agreement?"

"Yes, it's not unheard of." She shrugs.

"I don't understand."

"A non-disclosure agreement can be negotiated for the right price."

I rake my hair back. "Jesus," I mutter. "Is that really why you think they won't discuss Rob?"

Cruz nods.

We sit in a dense silence that's only disrupted by my sniffling.

She watches me as my eyes blink sheepishly at the glass table before me.

My cellphone vibrates on the tabletop, breaking our silence. I turn it over to confirm it's not Rob saying he's on his way home. I see a message from Cassidy that includes pictures from last night, of her smiling big in the costume she borrowed. I feel comforted by her smile and it grants me a genuine smile of my own.

Cruz glances at my phone with curiosity.

"Oh, it's just my baby sister," I offer, then flip my phone back over.

"Cassidy?"

"Yes." I shake my head and grin at her. "I forget you know almost everything about me."

Cruz smiles bashfully, looking down at her hands.

"Are you and Valletta more than partners?" I blurt out in an attempt to learn something about Adella Cruz and regain some balance between us.

"What? No!" Cruz answers, fighting laughter. "He's my partner, but we work separately sometimes," she says. "It's nice to have someone. We don't have...we're both the caretakers and responsible ones in our families, like you. So, he has my back and I have his. We're everything but lovers," her voice tender as she speaks of her chosen family.

My cheeks grow warm. Another heat wave travels through me, but instead of dissipating as before, it stays, resting in my abdomen. Nausea quivers my stomach. I stand, ready to bolt to the bathroom.

"Are you okay? You don't look so good."

"I'm fine. I just..." I stop before I explain that the morning-after pill I took can cause nausea. I fan myself with my hand. "I'm fine," I say again to soothe myself.

Cruz stands, clasping my hand in hers, and pulls me towards my back patio. She opens the glass door and I race past her. I lean forward onto the railing, resting my forehead on my folded arms. Savoring the cold air needling at the exposed skin of my legs, I wish I wasn't wearing this cashmere sweater.

"Better?" Cruz asks, standing next to me.

"A little," I moan pathetically from the crook of my elbow.

Cruz steps closer, then slowly lifts my sweater from my lower back. She then lifts the fabric above my bra strap, gliding her fingertips up my spine as she does this. My back now exposed to the chilly air.

"Better?"

"Yes," I answer.

The cool air is helping, but her touch claims all my attention.

She delicately swirls her fingertips on the exposed skin of my back in big circles, starting at the top, swirling down slowly, then starting at the top again. My skin tingles with goosebumps and my nipples harden from her touch.

"What was that? Panic attack?" she asks.

"No, I just had one of those and that definitely wasn't one," I reply, my mouth still muffled by my arm.

"You did? I've never had one."

"Well, let me tell you," I say with some humor as I turn my head to the side. "They're not fun!"

"I bet. Tell me about it." Adella leans closer as she continues to tickle my back.

I recognize that this is her cop brain talking me through what she believes to be a panic attack, but I indulge her. "I was leaving Chanel and my body grew unbearably hot and my heart pounded in my chest. The room was spinning so quickly that I couldn't keep my balance. And then I fainted." I leave out the throwing up portion of the story. Living through it once was horrifying enough.

"Ouch. What caused it?"

"I don't know," I lie. "You know my life as well as I do, I'm sure you can piece that together," I say, standing upright. My stomach does one threatening flip but subsides when I look at her face.

She steps closer, gripping my arms. "Are you okay? Not dizzy or anything?"

"No."

"No, you're not okay?" she teases me. Her full pink lips tighten with a playful smirk.

"Adella." I pause, watching her lips relax back to their perfect form. "May I kiss you?"

Her small hands cup my face, pulling my lips to hers. Instead of stiffening, my body slackens, relaxing into her. She wraps her arms around me, slipping her hands under my cashmere sweater, then pulls me tighter. Her fingertips caress my back, causing my nipples to harden again. I wrap my arms around her tiny frame, inhaling her scent. My kiss deepens and she allows my tongue to slide over hers. Adella dances her fingertips around my waist, slipping one warm hand under my bra, cupping my breast. She circles my nipple with her rough thumb, and I moan into her mouth.

I break from her perfect lips. "Come," I say, taking her hand in mine.

The thought of us in the bed I share with Rob consumes me, and it's all I want. All I can see.

Her feet remain firm. Her head down.

"Adella," I whisper, stepping in front of her. I place my palm on her cheek, and her mournful face rises. Her eyes crawl away from mine and towards the patio door.

"I'm sorry. This was a mistake," she says in a small, uneasy voice before turning sharply, then bolting for the patio door, swinging it open and leaving it open behind her.

I stand paralyzed for a moment until my mind shouts at me to run after her. I make it to my front door as Adella's car moves quickly, backing away from my home. I stand with my mouth open, watching her drive away as the world grows smaller, closing in on me. An entanglement of embarrassment and desire strikes me as her car turns the corner and is no longer visible. I'm frozen as shame creates a knot in my belly. I swallow the lump in my throat and totter through my open door, closing it and locking it.

Leaning against the large wooden door, I close my eyes, thinking of her perfect pink lips. Torn between the impulse to speed up and the intense alarm to slow down, I lift my hand, slipping it under my sweater, imagining her hand that was gripping my breast, circling my nipple. My tongue remembering the taste of her lips, I lift my skirt, sliding my other hand inside my panties. With each moan, I think of her lips, her eyes, her touch. The elation peaks, and as I rock myself back down, catching my breath, I ache for more. The bubbling desire only partially quenched, and my mind still packed with trepidation.

Removing my hands from under my clothing, I open my eyes to see a photograph of Robert staring at me, smiling. Walking back to the dining table, I glare at the framed photograph of him in Positano. I stop to gaze at his handsome face laughing at something I said while taking the photo. We were still so in love when this photo was taken. I hadn't fully realized my place in his world or what it meant to be his wife. I hadn't suspected him of cheating yet. My heart was happy then. The woman who took that photo was a happily married woman. I was Robert's wife and I belonged to him.

I wouldn't have dreamt of kissing another man, or woman, or falling for Ben, or attending the open house. What has become of me? Who is this woman who would kiss Adella Cruz?

Even with the excruciating pain Rob has caused me leaving me feeling unmoored, I have an annoying desire to be fair.

My mother always said, her voice wispy and sweet, "Choose kindness." Without warning, I respond with an ugly snort of laughter, jarring me from the tempering memory of my mother.

I carefully collect the frame from the table it rests on, glowering at Rob's smiling face. With it in my hand, I head to the garage, adding it to the box that delivered my morning-after pill that I'll be disposing of tomorrow. Closing it again, I smile, allowing my shame to be absorbed by the fiery rage I hold for Rob.

19

Puzzle Piece

I'm expecting Rob's arrival late this evening. The wife in me is excited to see him, but the new woman growing daily inside me is nervous for him to come home.

The night and its darkness creep in, bringing with it intimidating grey clouds that roll over the sky like a heavy wool blanket. There's a new chill to the air that only inbound rain can offer. Rumbling thunder sends tremors through the bones of the house and the night's coldness nips at my skin. I take my time strolling around my house, closing all open blinds. When I reach our bedroom, I choose an over-sized camel-colored Max Mara knit cardigan from my closet to wrap myself in.

Just as the long fingers of night choke what daylight is left, my doorbell hums, causing my spine to stiffen. I freeze in place, and like a frightened child with an overactive imagination, I want to hide. The eyes watching me through Rob's office window appear in my thoughts without warning, sending a shudder through my limbs that finishes in my belly.

Standing ten feet from the front door, I peek through the thick textured glass. I lean in slightly to gain better sight, but shadows hide the person's face. It's a man with a medium build and shaved head.

"Robert!" the unknown man rages.

My body stays where it is, feeling safer standing at a distance from the door. My thumb frantically spins my wedding ring in circles.

I glance at the alarm panel—it's still active. The man yells my husband's name again.

"What do you want?" I shout at the door, my voice noticeably shaky.

"I want Robert FUCKING Claire! Tell him to come out here, NOW!"

"He isn't here!" I shout back at the door.

Silence.

He places his head in his hands, still standing tall, as he begins weeping. The despair in his sobbing shocks me coming from a man of his size. He slowly runs his hands from his eyes backwards over his shaved head, resting them on his neck as he leans his large head back into them.

"Sophia?" He sounds tender now, wounded even. "I won't hurt you. I'm sorry. Don't be afraid," he pleads through my door, staring at my shape through the textured glass. "I just don't know what I'm doing anymore," he says while successfully holding back tears.

He rubs his shaved head and makes his way to a clear part

of the glass door that doesn't hide me. His icy blue eyes glimmer brightly when he finds me in his sight. It's the man from the football game. He rubs his eyes with his palms, causing them to redden further. His cheeks burn a rosy red as he sees me, cracking a smile that says *I won't hurt you.*

"What do you want?" I ask again, now looking him in his eyes.

"Sophia?" he slurs, squinting at me.

"Yes, who are you?" I tighten my sweater around my torso as I step closer.

"I'm Mark. Mark Coldwell."

The name sounds familiar.

"Do I know you?"

"Yes. Well, no. But I know you." My feet slide a cautious step away from the door. "No, wait! Please! Listen!" He's pleading again with his slurred, sloppy words. "My wife is Megan. Megan Coldwell. You and I met at the football game."

I remember him—the paranoid man with all the facts at the football game. But I also remember the news story about his wife's murder. She was the first. He found her in their home when he returned from a work trip. He's retired military. An article stated he specialized in security and surveillance while in the military, but he now works as a risk manager in the defense contracting sector of a firm called REAL. The firm specializes in major tactical and technological resourcing.

I step closer to the door to see him more clearly. His light blue eyes sad, full of desperation. I just don't know what he's desperate for.

"Why are you here?" I ask again, stepping closer to the door, watching his muscular jaw tense with my question.

"I," he laughs at what he is about to say, "I came to pay your husband a visit."

"Why?" We're now face to face with only thick glass between us. His shaved head dripping with rain.

He gazes down at me, a drop of water cascades off his sharp nose. "Well, I was planning on killing him."

His honesty shakes me in the oddest way. It's comforting.

"I won't hurt you, though, I promise. I just know *he* killed her." He closes his eyes, places his wet forehead on the glass door, as tears fall from his round tightened face.

"How? How do you know that?"

"Can we talk? I have things to show you." He stops crying abruptly, getting back to business.

"Are you drunk?"

"Very."

Again, his honesty is encouraging. I disarm my alarm to open the front door where the man waits to be let in.

He slides through the door gracefully for his bulky frame. His broad body built to protect. The heavy stench of liquor thickens the air around him. I bring him to the sitting room and offer him coffee or water, but he declines both.

I toss him a towel from my kitchen as we both sit, his eyes never leaving my face. I sit next to him on my oversized couch with my legs tucked to my side.

"Sophia," he jumps right in, slurring less, "I know this is going to sound crazy."

"Try me," I interrupt without thinking, daring him to test the limits of my current reality. He wipes his face with the small towel, removes his soaking wet jacket, letting it fall to my Kavi Collection rug, then hangs the towel around the back of his short thick neck. I notice his wrist tattoo again made up of a cluster of stars and its familiarity bothers me.

"Like I told you, I know your husband and my wife were having an affair. I know because I saw it. I saw the texts. I showed them to the cops," he says as he hands me a cellphone with the text conversation ready to be read. Detective Cruz had told me the first woman murdered had a husband who had proof.

"I would have forgiven her. I would have. I swear." He begins to drunkenly sob into his broad hands.

"These are texts between my Rob and your Megan?" I slide my hand unoccupied by the cellphone over the top of his to calm him, as I continue scrolling through the phone.

"Between them, yes," he says. His red eyes are still leaking as he raises his face from his palms and continues, "Talking about the sex they've had and the sex they want to have next. When I got home, when I found her, her phone had texts on it from him saying he was five minutes away. He was at my house that day!"

"Mark, that doesn't mean it was him." I shake my head as I continue to read the text messages on the dead woman's cellphone. Each text building the sexual tension between Megan and Rob. Each text making it painfully obvious what they were to each other.

He sits in silence, gawking at nothing. Sandy blonde stubble is sprinkled across his jawbone, contouring his tense muscles. His lids slide shut as he extends his palms down his denim-covered thighs.

"Her eyes were open when I found her," he whispers with his eyes still closed firmly. Silent tears falling into his lap when the vision of finding his wife plays in his head.

I stare at his trembling hands, now white knuckled from gripping his jeans so tightly, stretching his tattoo on his inner wrist. This man is ruined. His soul crushed. He loved his wife very much. There is nothing more painful than failing to protect the one you love. I also feel for him because I understand how betrayal can change the disposition of a person's nature.

"Sophia, you have to be careful. He is dangerous." He leans in, flicking his eyes open and setting them on my mouth and whispers, "He will kill you, too." His breath reeks of booze and cigarettes. I don't move away, but instead look up into his blue eyes now tunneling into mine. He continues, "You're like my Megan, so fragile. You have to run." His broad, sticky hand grazes my cheek.

"Mark, please." I turn away from his drunk rambling but remain seated. I redirect. "What is that tattoo? Is looks like the Subaru logo."

He titters. "Subaru, huh?"

I shrug and lift my brows playfully, proud that I'm managing him well.

"It's the Pleiades star cluster, which is actually what the Subaru logo is inspired from."

I slowly nod, feigning mild interest. A moment of silence passes.

Mark turns to me. "I don't want you to die," he mumbles.

I redirect and grasp control again. "You can't come here again. You understand? This was stupid! You're drunk and could have done a very foolish thing." I'm scolding him like a child, but he agrees.

With his head down after being scolded, he says, "I'm sorry about setting off your house alarm. I didn't mean to. I thought I knew what system—or the type—but I was wrong." He slurs his apology, but I hear it with expert clarity.

"That was you!" I shout at him with my spine now stiffened, but he keeps his eyes pointed at his feet.

He nods his head sheepishly. "Sorry," he says as he shrugs his heavy shoulders.

"Why were you watching me through the window?"

"I wasn't really. I—"

"I saw you," I declare thick with blame.

"I was watching Robert. Once the alarm went off, I lost track of where he was. So, I went back to his office, and that's when I saw you standing there wrapped in a white blanket. You looked so tiny in that large thing. Eyes frozen wide as you watched me watch you."

"I wasn't watching you, Mark," my voice peppered with annoyance, "I was trying to see *who* you were. All I could see was eyes."

"I figured as much since you didn't run from me at the football game," he chuckles. The sharp realization of just how bizarre my life is aches deep in my bones.

His ice blue eyes gloss over my face as his head tilts as if he's looking at a wounded puppy.

"What?" I ask, hoping he won't make me regret asking.

"It's just that I have more to tell you. You won't like it. I'm sorry." His apology laced with remorse causes his eyes to fall to his hands cupping each other in his lap. "I don't like hurting you."

My heart grows heavy with sorrow. The man in front of me has been more honest in the short moments I've known him than my husband has ever been. My heavy heart pounds in my chest with the unbroken wish for a genuine love from Rob.

"I told you at the football game that I know about Benjamin…I also know about the baby. I know you couldn't get pregnant with Robert." His tone offers a shocking tenderness one wouldn't expect from such a rugged looking man. His eyes meet mine as he says, "It must have been terrible for you to make that choice."

My gut tightens. "How do you know about that?"

"I was in security and surveillance. Special Ops."

"Was?"

"I have friends," he says with an unnatural smile.

"Hmm. What do you do now?" I ask, still circling my original question.

"I'm a risk manager." His hands remain cupped in his lap, but his demeanor has changed completely. He's cold and ready for interrogation.

"I don't know what that is."

"I manage risk," he answers, adding the same unnatural smile as before. His attempt at appearing playful comes across as robotic.

He's avoiding giving me the answer. Mark might have been trained in the military, but I've been married to the expert for years. Some are trained in how to avoid giving information, others are born with the gift.

"Okay," I say with a nod and pursed lips. While I'm not new to this game, I don't have the energy to burrow into Mark's armor.

Mark looks down and his eyes begin to dart erratically around the carpet beneath him. His chest begins to rise and fall quickly. Each breath grows with intensity as his eyes continue to shift in their sockets.

"Hey, are you okay?" I say as I lean towards him, too nervous to touch him.

His breath immediately slows, and his gaze drifts up from the carpet. His icy blue eyes now locked on mine, he says nothing.

"Are you okay?" I ask again.

"I knew about the affair. I hoped she would stop it. Or that he would," he says as if entering a conversation in progress. "She told him that she loved him," he says with his eyes still locked on mine.

I look away and fight the urge to ask if Rob said it back to her. Disgust fills me, causing a nauseating sourness to build in my throat.

I don't tell Mark about Detective Cruz because I don't trust his ability to be sensible. I don't offer much information at all. I just listen.

Ripping my phone from my hands, Mark makes a drunk, stubborn point of entering his number into my cellphone in case I need him. I watch him thumb at it frantically. His need to protect me is like any man who has gone through his pain; he needs to save someone because he was unable to save his woman.

After an hour, Mark's eyes begin to grow heavier with each word he speaks. I call him a cab instead of an Uber so there is not a digital record of a visitor leaving my home. Before sending him home to sleep off the booze and shower away the stench, I remind him to never come back to my house.

As I ready myself for bed, I think of Rob and rage sears through my veins. Not because of the details of the affair I heard for an hour—if not with Megan, it would be with someone else—but because of how utterly sloppy Rob is.

20
Closer

My body is only covered by the thick white cotton nightgown that hangs down to my ankles, blowing in the intense wind atop the building's rooftop. Facing Rob, whose face is no longer a serpent. His back is at the tall building's ledge, I step to him slowly, eager to embrace his tall body in my arms. The wind beats his tie against his face as I stop directly in front of him. A sweet, knowing smile curves my lips. Placing my hands on his abdomen, gazing up at his face, his eyes staring back down into mine. I lean in, hugging his large body in my arms, reaching my hand up around his neck, cupping it within my hand as I squeeze him in a loving embrace.

I pull away slightly, his tie now violently flapping against his back, and lean into his lips, pressing them softly against mine. His hands search my body, stroking eagerly over the top of my nightgown. I hold my lips to his, savoring his touch and taste as he fervently caresses my curves. He hurriedly lifts my nightgown up, yanking it above my waist to reveal my nakedness. As he holds it with one hand, the other reaches for his belt buckle, unfastening it eagerly.

The wind stops abruptly, allowing the night's air to grow eerily silent. I pull my lips from his and push my palms against his abdomen. Pulling away from him gently, allowing my nightgown to fall back to my ankles, our eyes stay locked on each other's. Rob's belt buckle hangs from the front of his pants, as his body remains hunched over from leaning down to kiss me.

Standing in front of him with a joyful smile, I say, "It was never going to be me," then abruptly shove him back. His balance betrays him as he falls over the ledge of the tall building, his terrified scream growing quieter as he falls to the city street below.

My eyes burn as I force them open. The peaceful sensation of the dream fills me, but as I force reality into place, the peace I feel in the dream veers into agitation. I shove the blankets off my damp body, then stand on my feet.

I sway to the bathroom, my eyes no longer burning. I splash my face with icy cold water, placing some in my palm, then cupping the back of my hot neck. I brush my teeth, attempting to shift into normalcy, but the emotions of the dream linger like the end of a bad cold that hangs heavy in the chest. Its tar-like substance coating the lungs, delivering a compact and centralized pressure.

I throw on my terrycloth robe, scrutinizing how it

hangs to my ankles and covers my arms, just as the thick cotton nightgown did in my dreams. I throw it off me as if it's on fire, allowing it to puddle on the large rug taking up my side of the closet. Instead, I pull out my favorite Christine Lingerie silk pajamas from a drawer, sliding my arms through the purple magnolia print, then button it up as my fingers shake. I then step into the matching pants, tying the waist. As I do this, I hit my hip bone with my fist, feeling a bonier version of my waist. Disregarding the strange sensation caused by what feels like foreign hips, I walk to the kitchen to make myself some coffee, hoping to shake this alarming, almost paranormal feeling hanging over me.

Turning the corner, I am startled to find Rob standing in our kitchen, thumbing at his phone. When I consider that he's most likely texting a female, my lips curl with disgust. Looking at his phone still, a slight smirk graces his mouth, triggering fire to run through my veins and my stomach to tighten with rage. He looks up at me, catching me off guard. His handsome face offers a welcoming smile. The rage continues to blossom through me as petty digs dance on my tongue but fail to launch.

"Hello, beautiful," his accent heavy as he sets his cellphone on our kitchen counter, face down, after locking it.

I force a smile and saunter to him. It is time to begin the game of pretending I don't see his deceit or exceptional lying. Normally, I'd begin deciphering what each movement meant: a flick of his eyes, a twitch of his lip, they were all fair game to be judged as a sign of his betrayal.

The game of interpreting Rob's methodical behavior was a game I rarely won. He is a good actor, and even if I won the game, I'm still losing. But my weary mind, jaded by the daily routine of this contest, ignores the invitation for the first time.

There are much larger doubts to agonize over at the moment. "When did you get home?" I ask, looking up at him. His face looks refreshed from his trip.

"Oh, I didn't want to wake you." He kisses me deeply, wrapping his arms around my waist, pulling me tightly to him. I wonder if he notices my thinning frame.

Pushing my palms against his chest, I offer him tea, which he declines.

The space between us grows larger with each passing secret I keep. I'm struggling for my best poker face—a game I was never good at.

I stare over the steam from the tea I hold at my lips as he reaches for his ringing cellphone. He silences it. I'm not even going to ask who it was. I don't want to hear another beautifully complicated lie.

"How was your trip?" I ask instead.

"Great! We had great success and I think Abe will be closing the deal soon." His chest noticeably expands with pride as he says with a chuckle, "I'm making Abe a richer man." His ego fills the room like a noxious gas.

I mumble, acknowledging his answer, as I stare out at Deep River and he continues explaining how "great" the trip was for Anexa. As I watch traffic, I try to shake the feeling still lingering from the dream. The sky shines a hue of purple, threatening a storm.

My phone ringing brings my mind back into my body and the room. Rob swipes my phone from the kitchen counter.

"Hello," his accent greets the caller. "Yes, may I tell her who is calling?"

Fuck, I think.

"Yes. Hold, please. Here, my love, it's Kelly" he says, holding my phone in the air for me to reach for.

My eyes are frozen wide. My face doubtful and confused. He's never jumped at answering my phone. Never. That would open the door for me to touch his phone.

"This is Sophia," I say, my eyes still frozen on him, wide with surprise.

"Sophia, it's Adella. Don't worry. I told him I was Kelly." I wondered who the hell Kelly would be when Rob asks.

"Hi, Kelly. How are you?" I ask, my muscles fatigued already from instant and overwhelming anxiety.

"If you can't, talk just say, 'Oh, I'm sorry. I don't have her number,' and we will talk later."

"Good. I'm well, thank you." Worried my knees might give in to the weight of my body, I sit at our dining table.

"Okay, listen. Benjamin Booth is not our guy," she says rapidly. Each word a jolt from her mouth to my ears. "Not only were we able to verify his alibi, but our warrant was approved to obtain his blood. Unlike all the other crime scenes, there was semen found in Abby Usher's bed. We will obtain a blood sample from Robert Claire to compare with the semen at the scene." She says Rob's first and last name, as if I wouldn't know that she is referring to my husband.

"Oh, that's great. I'm glad you're coming!" I say with an awkwardly forced smile while Rob's eyes stay securely on me. The silky deception rolls off my tongue surprisingly well.

Cruz continues, "Sophia, Robert is the only suspect. We must do Robert's arrest right. I can't have him and his attorneys…" Her voice fades away, then she murmurs, "It's him, Sophia. I was wrong before. I'm sorry," her tone apologizing for not protecting me and extends a deep warning.

"Yes, I'll see you there…yes. It starts at seven thirty. Thanks, Kelly!" I hang up the phone and wait to be questioned, but the questions don't come. I sense his dark eyes locked on the back of my head and I anxiously wait for him to speak.

He leaves the room, arriving back in a moment with a bottle of wine he had crafted with a local vintner. He fumbles with the cork, then moves unusually slowly to retrieve two glasses. Out of the corner of my eye, I catch him pause awkwardly over the now filled glasses.

He steps to me, setting a glass half filled with red wine in front of me. I glance up at his dark eyes, piercing me with an unfamiliar glare.

"For you…my love." He points at the mouth-blown Tiffany wine glass resting on the table in front of me.

"It's a little early for wine," I say, pushing it away with trepidation. I think, for a moment, how easy it would be for him to drug me if he wanted to.

Rob pushes the glass back towards me, sliding it closer than before, and says, "You really must try it."

I inspect the pale red liquid, detecting small chunks of debris at the bottom of my glass that could be typical wine sediment. He sits at the other side of the long glass table and swirls his wine. Gooey silence stretches across the long table. His spiteful gaze rests on me as he lifts the glass to his lips.

He tastes it, puckering his lips, and offers his opinion with a condescending smile. "It's almost like it's hiding something, but I can't put my finger on it." His eyes burrow into me, daring me to ask him if he is talking about me or the wine.

If paranoia weren't consuming me, I could think of something to say, something to do other than pick up the glass. But without an escape plan, my lips part as I raise the glass to them. I take a small sip, letting the red wine saturate my tongue.

His eyes never leave me, as if waiting for my response. I offer a kind smile after swallowing the tiny sip.

"So," he says, "did you have fun with Melanie while I was gone?" His eyes squinting now, daring me to answer from the other end of the table.

Does he know I didn't have dinner with Melanie and went to the open house instead? I choose to lie. That's what we do, isn't it? "It went well. You know Melanie, always something to say," I answer breezily. As if reading my mind, his questions continue.

"Oh, I *know*. Did you have any visitors while I was away?" His tone raises with expectancy while his eyes glower over the wine glass resting on his lips.

"Visitors? No," I answer as I press the corners of my mouth down, sluggishly shaking my head.

He squints at me with an exaggerated smile and says, "Cheers, my love." He raises his glass and waits for me to raise mine.

After I take another tiny sip, I try to remember what Fred said about the unique fentanyl Anexa created and how little is needed to kill a person. If my wine was poisoned, then I'd already consumed more than the fatal amount. Rob continues his relentless questioning, "Soph, wasn't Cassidy here?"

"Oh, yes! Silly me. She stopped by," I answer while touching my forehead in a display of forgetfulness. "How did you know?" I ask, waiting for the effects of the fentanyl to kick in: dizziness first, then confusion, followed by unconsciousness. My anxiety slides into panic as I grow hot and my legs tingle.

His eyes fall from me for the first time since he brought me the wine. They land on his hand resting on the glass table in front of him. "She called and asked for the new alarm code. She said she still has a key but didn't want to risk the alarm being set off," he answers with a tone reeking of annoyance that she still has a key.

"Yes, she stopped by because she was in town." Heat flushes through my body, causing wetness to pop from my pores. I quickly change the subject, ignoring his desire to press on. "Don't forget about the ball. I'd like you there to help by five o'clock; I need you by my side. Tuxedo, please," I demand, shifting control.

"As you wish, my love," he says with clear venom as he raises his glass in the air to toast with a smug smile. He then tilts his head back and gulps the remaining wine in one enormous mouthful.

He rolls to his feet, gliding to me, until he's standing above me. He points at my glass and asks, "Do you not like it?"

I shake my head slowly as my heart slams against my ribs. I keep my eyes on my wine glass resting on the table in front of me.

Rage simmers in his voice. "Fine," he says as he exhales

sharply, then scoops up my glass with one hand, tilting his head back again to take it all down. Setting the delicate wine glass down on the table in front of me, he growls, "Don't misjudge me, Sophia. That'd be a mistake."

I keep my gaze ahead of me, staring at the long glass tabletop, making sure not to look at him while staying mindful of his location. He hovers above me a moment longer, daring me to look at him, before he turns away, then storms out of the room. After a few moments, his car tires squeal as he speeds down our driveway. My body gradually moves back to normalcy, the strange sensations disappearing. A crushing fatigue that overturns any worry Rob had poisoned me replaces the strange sensations caused by my panic attack.

21

Twilight Zone

Rob and I politely dodge the brightly colored elephants in the room. Each one representing our own lies. We say hello in passing, but we are utterly broken. I wait for him to explain, I wait for an answer about the accusations by Cruz, but nothing comes.

I still haven't told Rob about the detective visiting—three times—or the other visitor, Mark. My marriage is a bizarre mirage of movements. I'm ready for it to crumble to the ground. I'm on edge, just waiting for something, anything to happen; for it all to come crashing down.

Rob has been a stranger, directing resentment at me, creating a nagging heaviness that he knows my various secrets.

I'm merely existing in this life. Floating through each day in a daze of mixed realities, with no mental energy to attend any of my meetings or lunches. I have an event this evening I'll have to pull it together for; it's for the children, after all. The woman I once was cared about that stuff.

Rob promised months ago he would attend this ball tonight, but he cannot be reached. I arrive alone and smile as if my perfect life isn't a complete sham. People ask how Rob is, I say wonderful and that he had to work. They ask where I've been, and I say I've come down with a series of colds but I'm on the mend now.

Candlelight reflecting off crystal stemware and decor creates a soft glow throughout the dim room. Each linen-covered table is decorated with tall centerpieces baring white fragrant flowers cascading from the tops.

After giving a speech to the seated black-tie crowd, I work the room by thanking the attendees and donors. The dim lights mix well with the romantic music and flowing drinks. What's a charity event good for if not the booze?

The string quartet pauses between songs just as the sea of faces parts slightly, allowing a handsome man to flow through. The handsome tan man with a chiseled jaw and perfect smile stands before me, his zesty citrus cologne thrills me, igniting an instant desire in my core.

"Sophia, hello. How are you this evening?" His voice monotone—almost robotic—as if he's forced to be here and it's past his bedtime. His wife hangs on his arm, smiling politely at me with her gold satin dress glistening in the soft light.

He extends his hand, prompting my breath to slip from me. My mouth opens, my mind reaches for words, any words, just as the string quartet begins to play "Waltz of the Flowers."

"Jacob Hope!" I finally say through the music. Sucking in

a deep breath, I extend my hand in return. He shakes it firmly.

"Have you met Sasha?" Acting the gentleman, he introduces his gorgeous wife Sasha, whom I've met before at networking events. She shakes my hand and confirms we've met. Sweetly, she compliments the event. I glance at Jacob again, taking him in, before glancing back at Sasha. His light blonde hair forces the memory of my fist tightening around a handful of it while his head was between my thighs.

"Your dress is lovely," her voice so soft, it almost gets lost.

"Thank you. Yours is beautiful as well. Gucci?" I ask.

"Tom Ford for Gucci," her airy voice politely corrects me, then she offers a sweet smile.

I return the smile as my mind continues racing with thoughts I don't dare share. I want to know, does his wife know about him, or is she like I was, completely oblivious to her husband's extracurricular actives?

"Give Robert my best," Jacob says with a dull smile, then takes his wife's hand, tucking it into his arm as he glides away abruptly.

I stand frozen for a moment watching them float away, melting in with the waltzing crowd of suits and gowns, while replaying all angles of the encounter: what it looked like to outsiders and questioning his wife's knowledge again.

Discomfort settles on my skin like an itchy blanket because the man has seen me orgasm. But the man who stiffly said, "Give Robert my best," was not the man at the open house. I've officially arrived in the Twilight Zone.

Upon arriving home, I see Rob's car parked in the garage. My heart drops into my stomach as the guilt creeps in and the weight of all I've done sits on my chest. My sanity seems to be something I can see, not something I possess.

Would Jacob tell Rob about what happened? Do they talk about it afterwards? Or is it, as my hostess said, "Maintain all activities here," followed by something about privacy? Would Rob be okay with it?

I'm wearing the guilt caused by my actions on my sleeve for everyone to see. I'm curious, how does someone like Rob or Jacob pretend so well? Or does one just get used to the emotional side effects of deceit?

Arriving home, I set my Tom Ford tote on the kitchen counter, then glance through the rooms and hallways on my way to our bedroom looking for Rob, but do not see him. His car is in the garage, so I know he's home. Walking past the sitting room, a flash of the faces who've visited its walls raid my mind. All the bizarre meetings held there almost register as normal now.

I slip out of my gown and into jeans, a long-sleeved V-neck top, and fetch a thick black jacket to search outside for Rob. Wrapping myself in the black jacket as I walk towards the backdoor, I stop to slip on my favorite Stuart Weistzman black leather heeled boots before exiting the warmth of my home.

I find Rob sitting on the back porch, drinking directly from a bottle of his wine in the moonlight. I see the metallic "RC" splashed across the soft black label. Of course, Robert Claire would be egotistical enough to name a wine he had made after himself.

"Hey," I say, strolling over to sit across from him. He ignores me. "The benefit went well. Jacob Hope says hello." He ignores me still. I stand to walk away, but he speaks, his words freezing me in place.

"I was served today," he announces solemnly with his shoulders slumped into his body.

"Served?" Apparently, we are doing this now. I sit back down.

"Yes, I did not give consent, but they served me today with a warrant to draw my blood."

"Rob, I don't know what you're talking about," I lie.

"Bullshit!" He stands and storms inside the house. I grab his empty wine bottle with my coat sleeve, then slip it into my coat.

I follow him. "Rob?"

"She told me she has been here! That detective bitch! You knew this whole time and didn't tell me?" His voice is thunderous, making me feel small.

"I…I didn't." I don't know what to say. I can't keep up with all the lies like he can. I'm trying to remember what he knows and doesn't know before I speak.

"Detective Cruz told me she warned you to stay away from me." My heart flutters at his wounded tone.

"Rob, I'm sorry. I didn't know what to do."

"Do you believe them?" He looks at me with wide eyes, searching my face.

I appease him by saying no.

"I did sleep with them," he confesses. I already knew about his affairs with the murdered women, but the words are still heavy on my heart. My stomach drops and it's hard to breathe.

"I know," I whisper, looking down.

"I don't know what's wrong with me." He begins to cry,

heaving powerfully. I walk to him, embracing him as he sobs.

"I wish our life could have been different together. I had such dreams for us," I say, stroking his coarse dark brown hair as he cries on my shoulder. "I really did love you. Through and through. The third time Cruz was here—"

"The third time?" His head rises, and he stops sobbing, his eyes puffy and watery still. "What do you mean, 'third time'?" He turns, taking a few enraged steps away from me.

"The third time," I confirm with a nod. Then with a stern smile, I add, "You murdering psychopath." I'm taunting him when he is at his lowest and it fills me with glee. My pulse hammers at my temples from excitement.

His face flushes white, then red before he charges in my direction. He stops right before plowing into me. "You betrayed me! For what?" he shouts into my face. The mist of his saliva settling on my cheeks.

"Oh, that's fucking rich. I'm the one doing the betraying?" The sarcasm spills joyfully from me. The color of his eyes now drowned by the blackness of his pupils as he raises his hand to strike me.

He darts his hand at my torso, "I'll fucking end you," he sneers, gripping my arm tightly. My skin burns, and I know there will be bruises. I remember the woman in his office, Brooke, reciting those exact words backs to him when he pinned her to the wall.

"It could have been different, you know. All of it." I smile again, mocking his vulnerability. He strikes his heavy open palm across my face. My stinging cheek is muted by the overwhelming feeling that my left eye may burst from its socket.

Reaching for my hair, he yanks on it, forcing my ear to his mouth. "I. Will fucking end you," he repeats, letting raw hatred spill from his lips. The heat from his breath warms my ear.

It's all too much. This nightmare my life has become breaks the remaining delicate strings of my mind. I begin to laugh. I know I sound mad, but my rib cage bounces relentlessly with each surprising laugh. He releases me, stepping backward slowly with a glare of disgust and confusion twisting his handsome face.

Still laughing uncontrollably, as tears spill down my cheeks, I snatch my tote and run to Rob's car. Turning the key, forcing the engine to roar to life, I press the door lock button just in time for him to reach the driver's side door. After repeatedly yanking on the handle unsuccessfully, he crashes a fist onto the window, but the glass remains strong. My heart pounding against my ribcage allows me to realize I've stopped laughing. Slamming the shifter into reverse, I crash my foot down onto the accelerator, causing Rob to tumble to the hard garage floor. I slam my foot down on the brake, the tires shrieking to a stop. His car now pointed towards our long driveway, I knock the shifter into gear. Rob is already at the passenger side window, pounding his fist even harder on the glass.

"SOPHIA!" he roars, his voice booming with anger, and for the first time I see the man Detective Cruz had warned me about.

As I drive away, he chases me to the end of the driveway, yelling for me to stop.

After a blink of a drive, I find myself restless, sitting on the corner of a hotel room bed. My hands fidget as I gnaw on my nail beds. I've already called Detective Cruz and described the fight Rob and I had. She told me to take pictures of any bruises or markings and text them to her, and that we'll make a report in the morning.

It's 11:30 p.m. and the city of Deep River is fast asleep. I used my debit card from a separate account in my maiden name, an account Rob doesn't know about, to get this hotel room. There isn't much money in the account, but it's enough. It is my money and I wasn't co-mingling it with some spoiled man-child who repeatedly screws over the one who loves him most.

I crave an escape. I want to feel something, anything other than the slow, painful moments of time. I wish for a fierce moment to shake me from this hell. I need something to be real—nothing is real anymore.

Fumbling for my cellphone, I begin to thumb through my contacts. I come across my sexy twin, Veronica, or simply V, as she added herself in my phone before I left the open house.

I text her.

She answers, offering her address.

Her house is in a newer, posh development. The development is grand in the way only newness can bring, each lavish home with unique architecture and impressive landscaping to match. Her home overlooks an empty field that's kissed by moonlight. She has styled it well with beautiful things. It's like her, understated but exquisite.

She gives me a tour of the beautiful house as if we are old girlfriends, sashaying casually with her bare feet that have toenails painted red. Her silky knee-length black dress accentuates her curves, leaving little to the imagination.

We stand on her enclosed second story balcony overlooking the moonlit field as cool air bites at the skin left exposed by the blanket we have wrapped around our shoulders.

"Would you like anything to drink? Party favor?" she offers flirtatiously.

"No, thank you," I decline, remembering the wicked hangover those "party favor" pills tender.

We stand side-by-side, taking in the beauty the bright moonlight offers on this cold night. She nudges me with her shoulder. "Did you want me to invite Jacob tonight?" I can feel my cheeks burn at the thought of repeating my night at the open house. "Or someone new?" She tosses her brown curled hair over her shoulder, allowing her spicy perfume to waft through the air.

I offer her a sly smirk.

"I didn't know you were into what Rob is. Rarely do the wives even know, let alone attend the parties."

She's wearing the pin I saw on Rob's desk made up of the symbol. The symbol I've seen at the open house, on the flyer, and in Maui. I glide the tip of my index finger over it as it glimmers in the moonlight. "Have you got your pin yet? You're a part of the group now," Veronica says as she bumps her hip against mine teasingly.

I smile and gaze out at the field. "Do you know Rob well?" I ask nervously, hoping I'm not crossing some line in the rule book, or revealing Rob has no clue I'm prowling in his secret life.

"Well, 'know,' no. I've partied with him before, though." She slides closer and kisses me. "You're a very lucky woman," she giggles.

"Do you party with him a lot?" I should have known they've been together; she is beautiful. What's left of my heart sinks into my stomach as she explains.

"Only once. About a month ago. I'd *love* to have both of you," she purrs as she leans into me.

I clear my throat. "May I please have that drink now?"

She nods, then begins the short journey to her kitchen. I follow, tossing the blanket we shared on her couch.

She pours us each a drink in short crystal glasses.

"Cheers!" She lifts her drink to toast.

"That party favor, may I?" I request the pill with a grin before reaching for my glass.

She winks and says, "Of course." Setting down her full, untouched drink.

Just as Veronica walks out of the kitchen to retrieve the party favor, I lean over the immaculate stone counter and pour four times the amount of fentanyl needed to kill a human—the vial I stole from Anexa—into her drink. I carefully close the vial, making sure not to let any of it touch my skin. I move away swiftly, sliding back into the space I occupied when she left, just as she floats back into the kitchen.

I study her in a flash. She holds the type of natural beauty that would make other women envious. The type of woman who doesn't need to place effort into her appearance, but when she does, she is utterly striking. I admire her and am proud she is the last woman I'll kill because she's quite memorable.

"Here," she says, leaning across the kitchen island, causing her spicy perfume to dance into my nostrils again. She sets down the tiny pill: this one white with a heart imprint on it.

I raise my glass. "I want to thank you for being memorable."

"Aww," she says in a cutesy way before slanting the glass to her lips, taking it all with one large gulp.

"May I use your ladies' room?" I ask.

She points down the hall with a slight puckered face from her drink.

I take my time in the bathroom: I pee. Wash my hands. Powder my nose and carefully reapply lipstick, being careful not to touch anything in her home with my bare hands.

Using my sleeve again, I reach into my oversized tote and pinch the empty bottle of wine Rob was drinking directly from when I arrived home. I open the bathroom door, saunter into the kitchen, and gently set his empty bottle into her garbage can, proudly displaying his initials in metallic letters on the black label.

Glancing up from the garbage can, I see her legs stretched on the kitchen's tile floor, peeking out from behind the center island. I hear her gurgling as one leg flops a little.

I take the glass that I touched, pouring the alcohol down the sink, then carefully place it in my tote. Before leaving, I make sure I wipe any surface I may have touched. I need to hurry; I must switch cars while Rob is still asleep.

22

Reasonable Remorse

I wind through the backroads of the city in my car after carefully and quietly returning home to switch cars. I tighten my grip around the steering wheel in anticipation, thankful the main roadways are not blocked at this hour by the protestors. The full moon in Taurus sits high in the night sky as I toss Veronica's glass out the car window, hearing it smash into a million little pieces. I know Ben is alone. I'm excited to see him. Though he doesn't know it yet, he will be excited to see me, too. My fingers stiffen on the leather that enfolds my steering wheel as my headlights flash across the small wooden billboard that displays Ben's apartment community name.

After being fired, he sold his grand home. His apartment is new—like most are here—but it is still an apartment, and that's something he would have been embarrassed of. I park my car in a designated visitor parking spot, then walk to his building, adjusting myself along the way.

I climb the stairs of building D slowly, stopping at the second floor where his door awaits my nervous knuckles. I stand for a moment to calm myself, adjusting my clothes one more time, remembering my purpose for being here: If I'm here with Ben, neither he nor I can be associated with Veronica's death. Rob will have been alone all night after fighting with me, just as I documented with Detective Cruz.

It's perfect.

I knock lightly, questioning if it was too light for him to hear.

I wait in the darkness on his doorstep.

I knock lightly again.

He rustles from inside the apartment, making my stomach dance with excitement.

He's at the door, and I suspect he's peering through the door's peephole. He takes longer than I thought he would to open the door once he saw it was me. I wait uncomplaining, glancing away from the door.

The deadbolt slips, and the door peels away from its weather stripping. He stands silent, groggy from sleep. His tousled hair a perfect mess and his body only covered in dark navy pajama pants hanging low on his hips. His handsome face dusted with dark stubble and wrinkled from sleep.

"Is that really you?" he croaks through lingering drowsiness.

I smile, the moonlight allowing him to see the nod of my head.

He moves out of his doorway in a hurry to wrap his arms around my body, locking my arms awkwardly at my side, causing my Tom Ford tote to drop from my hand. "I'm so glad to see you," he sighs in my ear, still squeezing me. He releases me, quickly bending down to pick up my tote. With my tote in one hand, he reaches for me with the other. We walk together into his apartment, hand-in-hand.

The moonlight offers shadowy light in his dark apartment. I stay standing by the front door as he sets my tote on a wooden table across the small room. There's a large, framed painting of a knight riding a horse holding a chalice in his right hand that swallows a small wall. Other than that, the walls are bare.

"Come in," he whispers.

I stay standing firmly in place. I have a plan. I'm in control.

But he still makes me feel unsteady, just like he did the first day we met. His bare chest baring that thick diagonal scar kissed by scattered moonlight only magnifies my unsteadiness.

His bare feet step to me and he grips my right hand, pulling me off the linoleum of the small square entryway and onto the carpeted floor. He peers into my eyes and my unsteadiness turns into tension as I try to fight the vulnerability bubbling under my surface.

I squeeze my eyes shut, trying to block out the emotions that threaten to come crashing, focusing on the reality of why I'm here.

Ben pulls me closer to him, causing his packed chest muscles to flex. I catch myself by placing one hand on the skin of his chest with the considerable scar, triggering a wave of heat to spread through me. I lower my head as I fight the image of Veronica's leg flopping from behind her kitchen island.

"What is it?" Ben asks sweetly.

Guilt floods my body, forcing me to feel the unfamiliar weight of authentic remorse. But then I remember what Ben had said to the police and I easily push away the discomfort and focus on my task.

He gently raises my chin with his bent index finger. His features bend to offer me compassion and love as he cups my face between his palms and places his lips on mine. Breaking from my lips, he reaches under my arms to embrace me. "I'll wait for you there alone." He whispers the lyrics in my ear as he squeezes me tighter against his bare chest.

He kisses me again, pressing his body against mine, allowing me to feel his hardness. I allow his kiss to excite me. His tongue glides over mine, prompting my chest to rise and fall with increased excitement.

His throat swallows hard as he skates his hand down between my thighs, deliberately sliding his stiff fingers up and down over the top of my jeans. My body sags as I release a sharp gasp.

Pulling my blouse over my head, he drops it to the floor, then reaches for the top button of my jeans, popping it undone. Then the second, and the third. Allowing him room to slip his hand into them.

Circling with his fingertip, my knees weaken, a low growl slips from his lips as he feels my tightness pulse around his finger. I grip his naked shoulders, clinging to his torso as his hand works faster, bringing me to the edge.

He tugs his hand out of my jeans, his eyes burning with excitement as he yanks them down in one swift, turbulent motion. He stays crouched down, purposely setting his hot breath between my thighs. The hot, moist air causes my head to fall back and my body to stiffen with anticipation.

He brings his hot breath to my skin, nudging his tongue on me. I cry out and my knees finally give in as I brace myself on his shoulders. He rises to his feet, scooping me up securely in his strong arms.

Laying me on his couch, watching me with quickening breath, he reaches down to untie the string of his pants, releasing them to fall at his feet. I spread my legs wide, allowing him to crawl over me. Ben braces his arms on either side of my head, pressing himself against me, delaying his urge to enter. He lifts his head above my bare breasts then kisses my tightened nipple. I reach down with greed, guiding him into me, causing Ben to gasp at the pressure of my touch.

My throbbing need escalates, wishing for him to press past my entrance, to release my desire for him, to bring me to the place where reality doesn't exist, only ecstasy.

Ben raises his hips upward, pulling himself away from me and out of my grip.

"Tell me how bad you want me," he demands.

I answer with a moan. A burning need for control rises deep from within me as I reach for him again, the pressure between my thighs now consuming. "Please," I beg, wrapping my legs tightly around his ass, attempting to draw him down, but his back remains arched.

Ben clutches a hand full of my hair, sharply pulling my head to the side, running his tongue up my neck until his mouth reaches my ear. "Tell me," he demands again.

Releasing my hair, his arm muscles swell as he lowers

himself down, sliding slowly inside me. Just before I feel all of him, just before I acquire the relief I'm desperate for, he begins to withdraw.

I let out a loud, needy groan and bite my lip. He sits back on his thick, muscular legs, watching me writhe with desire for him. "Ben," I whine with need, and reach for him, my back arching involuntarily.

He leans to his side, quickly swiping something from the coffee table. With a strong flick of his wrist metal glides effortlessly across metal. Ben points it at me. I can see the sharp blade gleaming in the moonlight. He keeps the knife pointed at me as he again positions himself between my legs.

Pressing the cold, sharp blade to my neck, his free arm braces his body above me. His hardness again pressing against my entrance. The pain from the blade breaking my skin is muted by him sliding into me; slowly and firmly, finally filling me completely. A groan escapes his throat as he feels me enclose around him.

Moving his hips with restraint, he holds the knife to my throat. "I missed you, Soph," he says with his hot cheek rolling against mine with each slow roll of his hips. He presses the blade harder on my throat as he slows his hips to a stop.

I moan in protest, tightening my legs around him to draw him closer, craving to feel him move. My pulse races as sweat beads on my dewy forehead.

"Tell me you missed me," he demands, the knife digging into my flesh. His face hovering motionless over mine.

"I missed you. Now get that fucking knife off me," I pant as I roll my hips against his.

His face relaxes as he kisses me, releasing the knife, letting it fall open to the carpeted floor.

"Fuck me," I demand, gripping his hardened arms, digging my nails into them. He lets out a sharp hiss from the discomfort.

Ben abruptly maneuvers me until I'm straddling him. "Fuck *me*," he commands, attempting to shift the power.

I roll my hips, grinding them against his. His moans, telling me I'm winning, even though I'm following his orders.

I reach down, gripping the still open knife, then place it against his throat as I continue bucking my hips. Ben thunders out a moany protest but allows me to hold the knife at his throat.

His broad hands grip my hips, using his powerful arms to quicken my pace. My nails grip the sweaty flesh of his chest as my eyes roll back in ecstasy when he pulses from deep within me. My head snaps back, and I let out a cry.

He lets out a sharp breath of discomfort; the blade had cut too deep. He swats at my hand violently, the blade soars from my grip, landing on the carpeted floor across the room. In one swift movement, Ben scoops me up and tosses me onto my clammy back.

His teeth grit at the sight of my naked body waiting for him. He reaches up to his neck, wiping away the blood caused by my lack of control.

Hovering above me, his arms now shaking at either side of my head. He presses his bare chest against mine, resting his lips on mine as he grips the flesh of my leg, lifting it to his side. His breathing ragged as he slams forward, filling me again, forcing another loud cry deep from my throat. Our skin slaps together as he quickens his pace.

His hands balling into fists, he releases a roar as he pulses powerfully inside me. I let out a cry as my mouth drops open from the pressure finally being released. The elation peaks as we both slow our movement.

Our hips now still as he lies on top of me. My heart still throbbing in my chest, with his competing. Our labored breath slows as we float back down together.

He lifts his head, his face above mine, placing his lips to mine.

"I'm sorry, Soph," he says meekly. I close my eyes, wondering if he's referring to throwing me under the bus with the police. He shifts to his back, moving me to his side. I tuck myself under his arm and swing my leg across his, then wiggle my body as close as it can be to his.

We lay together: motionless, silent, sticky. Letting time pass with my head resting on his chest.

My finger slides across his dense, thick scar. Carefully orbiting where his skin grew back together, healing itself from the abuse it had taken. His chest rises and falls smoothly, his heart finally catching a calm pace.

I continue caressing the uneven, raised skin of the large scar, shutting my eyes tightly. I grow weary straining to hold on to whatever goodness is left inside me before the darkness pulls me under completely.

Ben lifts my chin from his chest and presses his lips to mine. His deep kiss numbing all worry and fear. He shifts his weight, rolling onto his feet, then reaches his hand out for me to follow. As I do, he grips my hand, then leads me down the hallway into his bedroom.

This is perfect. Even the neighbors will say they heard us all night.

23

The Actress

My hotel room curtains are closed, blocking the morning sun from fully assaulting my eyes. I eagerly reach for my phone to see if there's been a new addition to the body count.

Nothing yet.

Veronica's body has yet to be discovered.

I have one missed call from Mark Coldwell, but no voicemail. A text from Ben that says he misses me already. Then, lastly, a missed call and voicemail from Detective Cruz. She asks that I make my way to her office to submit a statement about my fight with Rob. She should be close to arresting him, finally. I've all but handed him over on a diamond encrusted platter. Veronica's corpse with an empty bottle of his private wine with his fingerprints on it should help. That is, if the semen I placed in Abby's bed didn't do the job. The night Rob left Abby's house, after he came home and fucked me, then fell asleep, I paid her a visit.

I must admit, for a while I was easily manipulated and controlled. I was the queen in his game of chess, whom he was willing to sacrifice for a more favorable position. I fell for his charm. I was sold on what our life was supposed to be, even though it would never happen. I foolishly believed in the dream of a perfect marriage. Hell, if we had children, I might have even put up with his bullshit. Yet, he managed to take even that away from me. He's taken everything from me, leaving me with nothing but him.

Nothing but him, his ego, his whores, and his lies.

What was I supposed to do? I'm done being the victim. I'm the queen in the game, goddamnit. I am the most powerful piece and I've made my move.

I'm done walking into rooms and receiving glares from women who fancy Rob, or even worse, the shame of walking into a room and being greeted with empathy from the other wives. I refuse to be that woman any longer.

I am thankful, however. Extremely thankful; he's taught me so much over the years. Mostly how to manipulate people into doing and seeing as I wish. I'm not quite as good as he is, but I'm close. This skill has helped me get close to the women he was sleeping with to kill them with Anexa's exclusive designer drug and frame him.

What I have in store for Rob will allow me to keep all we have. He will no longer be my embarrassment. With him gone, I can remarry and have children. I can have the life I deserve, the life I planned for.

Not only did Rob unintentionally teach me how to engineer

myself and my words to sway people and situations, but I also absorbed details about his businesses and their transactions—including information about drugs such as fentanyl. He's an intelligent man, my husband. That is, when he isn't thinking with his dick. It will be exhilarating to utilize all the knowledge I've acquired once he's gone.

To be clear, I didn't want to kill anyone. What I *wanted* was a happy marriage, and if that wasn't available, a divorce with a happy divorce settlement. I didn't want to hurt anyone. I always felt undecided right before each girl and guilty afterwards. It got easier, though. Listening to them talk about my husband like he belonged to them. Listening to them cry. Listening to them be apologetic or dare to be unapologetic as their voices burned with possession. Then, finally, listening to their throat gurgle for air as it folded in on itself.

Sadly, I didn't have the pleasure of watching Rosey Franklin. It was a happy accident seeing her drink waiting next to mine at Starbucks, with her name written delicately on the cup of tea. She was giggling on the telephone as I dropped the liquid into her tea. The bitch had just left Rob's office and was on her way home. It was risky. There could have been people watching, or worse, cameras. But I was careful, diligent to avoid being seen. You see, even the most carefully planned projects take on some risks.

I only killed the ones who knew about me, though. That's how I decided. I couldn't kill them all; there are far too many, but I need a healthy body count to make sure Rob appears gruesome and easily hated. Each girl who died knew he was married, and each paid their price while helping me frame Rob.

I ready myself to visit Cruz, making myself presentable, but also attempt to appear as if I've been through hell. This isn't a hard task; I still have sapphire blue crescents under my eyes and my olive skin has a strange grey hue to it. Before leaving my hotel room, I slap, poke, and pinch any bruises to accentuate them.

Detective Cruz stands impatiently in the waiting area of the police station with her hands held together behind her back. Her hair is slicked back tightly and she's wearing another grey, slightly baggy pantsuit that hangs from her petite frame.

In the seats near her, men and women in handcuffs sit together in silence. Their eyes red and swollen from what I assume is pepper spray used during crowd control at a protest. She greets me with a single nod in place of a smile and escorts me to her office. We pass Valletta in the hallway; his eyes scan me from feet to eyes, pausing hard on my eyes. No smile. No greeting.

Once in her office, Cruz informs me they've collected Rob's blood to test against the semen found at Abby Usher's. She claims they will have solid cause to arrest and charge him by tonight.

The corners of my mouth start to curl into a smile when she shares this information. I fight the smile but it's coming with intensity. I hang my head and reach for something deep inside to bring the correct emotions for this moment. My parents— their accident—I think of their lifeless bodies having to be peeled from the distorted metal object that was once their car, causing the tears to flow with ease. I raise my head to display my impressive tears. Cassidy may have been the musician, but

I was always the actress.

Detective Cruz stands, reaches for her office door, closing it to offer me privacy to weep. She sits in the chair next to me, offering her usual kindness and sympathy. I am comforted again by her scent. She is such a strong, intelligent person, but her vulnerability towards me creates a strange mix of security and desire. While she doesn't admire the real me, it's still comforting having someone like her on my side.

"I didn't think you were right, detective," I sob. "I couldn't believe it. I wouldn't. What will happen now?" I daintily dab at my eyes with a tissue.

This will be the last time I'll have to appear to be the sad, broken wife to her. The last time I'll have to cry tears for her benefit.

"I know," she rasps. "You need to stay away from him and the house, at least until we arrest him."

I nod in agreement and say, "Okay. I will."

She slides a paper across her desk, stopping it directly in front of me. She then sets a basic black pen next to it.

"What do I say?" I ask, reaching for the pen.

"Just write down what happened last night," her voice smooth and comforting. She places her hand on top of mine, tenderly stroking it with her rough, unmanicured thumb.

I give a slight smile to signal that I understand her request. However, the story of what happened last night is not what I'll be describing.

I begin to fill out the blank statement form by writing my name, address, and phone number. Above the written statement section there is a line that reads, *I, the undersigned, make the following statement voluntary, without threat, duress or promise of reward.* I focus on the words "promise of reward" before I begin.

I take my time perfecting the narrative, creating perfect loops in cursive.

Cruz rests back in her chair, then leans to her right, opening a drawer while I continue focusing on writing the story that I need told. She removes a large digital camera and sets it upon her desk. Once I'm content with the statement I've written for her, I raise my chin and meet her dark brown eyes.

"Are you ready?" she gestures to the digital camera as she stands. "I know you sent me photos, but I should take some while you're here."

I nod, pushing the statement to the middle of her desk, then setting the pen on top of it.

"Over there, please." She motions to a bare wall. I follow her directions.

She takes the first picture, then pauses, glancing at the screen, measuring the instant feedback the screen provides. Happy with her work, she moves closer to me and continues taking pictures. "Turn your head to the left. Push your hair behind your ear," her voice professional and curt. She stops just in front of me with her head tilted downwards as she studies the camera's LCD screen. I watch her approve the photos, noticing that her jaw muscles are tightened.

"Okay," she says, then turns to walk back to her chair tucked behind the large desk.

I follow her lead, taking a seat.

She examines my statement, her eyes scanning the page

quickly. Lifting only her eyes, she says with surprise, "You were with Benjamin Booth last night?"

"Yes," I answer coldly.

Cruz looks at the statement again, then back to me. "All night?" Her tone lowers.

"Yes."

Leaning back in her chair, her gaze fixes on me, but she remains silent.

"Is the statement sufficient?" I ask, hoping to move through this sticky moment.

Her eyes blink rapidly as she answers, "Yes, Sophia. It's adequate." She crosses her arms, struggling not to show emotion.

"Thank you. Thank you for all of it," I say with sincerity.

"I'll be in contact once we arrest him. Stay away from the house and Robert until I call you," she snaps, then stands abruptly. "Can I walk you out?"

"Oh, no. That's not necessary," I answer as I stand, collecting my purse.

She forces a smile.

As I walk out of her office, I resist grinning at the knowledge that she's burning with jealousy over me spending the night with Ben. My connection with Cruz was fun and exciting and I would like to explore it further, but I needed Ben for my alibi. It's time for Adella to say goodbye.

Driving back to the hotel, I go over in my head exactly what will happen now. I'll inherit all his company shares per his shareholders' agreements. I'll receive all real estate, including our home—I'll receive all assets. I'm his wife, after all, and Washington is a community property state. I'm sure the shareholders will want to buy me out of Anexa, as well as any other business I might own interest in. This is part of my plan, though, and I welcome any offers from the shareholders. The cash will be more than enough to start over, free of Robert Charles Claire and his pompous family.

Anexa will be announcing it's going international and tonight all my planning will pay off. I'm filled with bubbly excitement because today is the day I've been waiting for.

Stepping into our home, its quiet rooms offer air only disrupted by the low hum of appliances and central heat. It's quiet in the way that makes hair stand like tiny needles protruding from the skin. The type of quiet that can shake a person in a way no alarm can. I take in these last still moments before the chaos.

I pour myself a glass of wine and take a big gulp. Flipping through my Facebook feed on my cellphone, I see an article posted by our local news about Anexa. It displays a photograph of Abe Brown, Rob, and others involved with the company going international. The article praises Rob for bringing more jobs to the area, which is just the politically correct way of saying more money. Yes, he is making big moves and making a lot of people rich, including myself.

Setting my still full glass of wine on the kitchen counter, I whisk it off with the back of my hand, causing it to crash into the wall, splashing wine and glass across the floor and wall. I leisurely stroll through our home and continue making it appear as if there was a significant scuffle with a broken vase here, a shattered picture frame there.

My doorbell hums. I am, again, frozen by its sound. Goosebumps surge down my legs and up my arms. I hide, ducking behind the wall, so whomever is at the door cannot see me.

"Sophia?" a man's voice calls. I remain hidden. He knocks on the door. I cringe at the thought of Ben showing up on my front doorstep. I've wounded him in unforgiveable ways, but I can't let him be an unpredictable variable in *this* plan.

"Sophia, it's Mark Coldwell. We met the other night, remember?"

Remember? He's got to be fucking kidding. Of course, I remember! How can I forget a man who shows up at my house completely drunk claiming he's there to murder my husband?

He repeatedly rings my doorbell and says my name louder and louder. He sounds drunk again.

I'm infuriated. This drunk moron is going to foil months of my planning. There's no fucking way I'm letting that happen. With an annoyed huff, I reveal myself to him by slowly stepping into view. He sees me and speaks my name again, but with lightness.

"Mark, you have to go! Rob will be home soon."

"I know, I know. That's why I need to talk to you right now. It's important!"

"Mark, leave. Now." I step closer to the door. Plant my feet firmly on the marble of my entryway.

"But there are plans for you tonight. I have to tell you!" he yells. Then in a hushed manner, he says, "I tried calling you, but you didn't answer."

"What? What plans?" I can only imagine the man has

plunged deeper into madness since failing to protect his wife.

"Trust me. Open the door, I have to talk to you."

I hesitate.

"Sophia, please." Again, his obvious desperation is irresistible.

I open the door and his shoulders drop with relief. He strolls through the doorway, pushing past my body. He radiates a calmness he was missing a moment ago, as if a switch was flicked.

"What is it, Mark?" I question as I close the door.

"May I have a drink?" he asks while looking around, eyeing the beautiful mess I've made.

"Yeah," I say with annoyance, then walk to the kitchen, as he follows.

"What is it, Mark? We really must hurry. Rob—"

He interrupts, "I know. He will be home soon. Which makes this perfect. He deserves this." He continues to look around at my redecorating: the wine glass on the floor complete with wine on the wall. Crystal vases and glass from picture frames shattered across rooms. He looks behind him at a hole in the wall and then down at the floor where the statue that made the hole lay. He doesn't say anything about the mess. Instead, he ignores it, launching a vicious scowl at me.

"It's you," he says through a tight smirk.

"It's me?" I raise my brows and shake my head with confusion.

"I thought he would hurt you, like he hurt the others. So, I followed you, you know, to stop him. That's when I found out it was you."

"Are you drunk again?" My mind instantly goes to discrediting him. A move Rob would appreciate.

"It's been you this whole time. I saw you last night, at Veronica Sutton's house. I shared your location when I entered my number in your phone. I saw what you did. I watched you leave in his car. It's been you this whole time."

He creeps closer to me.

I step away.

"Mark, I don't know what you think you saw but—"

"DON'T FUCKING PATRONIZE ME!" he belts so loudly my body winces.

I put my hands out to calm him while stepping away slowly, but his bulky body follows.

"You killed my Megan and you're trying to make it look like it was your husband, you clever little bitch." His upper lip curls.

I stagger backwards to run, but Mark grips a handful of my hair and twists, setting my scalp on fire. He slams my body into the wall with little effort, causing me to crash into it with a tooth-knocking thud. I let out a pained wail as my body falls freely to the floor, slamming the air from my lungs on impact.

As I fight through the haze consuming my vision, he advances, climbing on top of me. His weight pinning my legs. His solid hands squeezing tightly around my neck. His plump thumbs press firmly on my throat. My esophagus fights to suck in air, but the force of his fingers won't allow it. I try kicking, scratching, but his determination triumphs. His eyes dance across my face with excitement as he watches me fade. Tiny white globes take up more and more of my vision. A ringing in my ears blends with my slowing heartbeat. My consciousness slips, and I stop fighting. I give in to the overwhelming fatigue.

It's not how I imagined death, but it's not the worst.

24

No More Secrets

Everyone thinks about how they might die. Chances are it's going to be something the body betrays its owner with, like heart disease or cancer. Being choked to death never crossed my mind.

My jaw aches as I quickly realize I'm feeling pain, which means I'm not dead yet.

My teeth knock together and my cheek feels as if tiny blades slice across it.

I'm slapped again but the pain is reduced due to the now numb skin on my cheek.

I peek, opening my eyes slightly to find Rob's frantic face above me. My head resting in the nook of his bent knee as he says my name repeatedly. Pain slices across my cheek again, forcing me to mumble, showing I'm conscious.

"What happened?" I whistle through an agonizing tight

throat.

"He attacked you," Rob reports, pointing to Mark's body lying on the floor next to me. Blood flows freely from Mark's cleanly shaven head. "I think I killed him," Rob reports with concern.

"Did you check?" I moan, gripping the rug beneath me to pull myself up onto my bottom.

"Check?" Rob looks at me puzzled.

"Check if he's dead?" I confirm my words.

He leans over, checking for a pulse on Mark's neck. "He's still alive," Rob reports.

"You have to kill him, Rob."

"What?" His eyes flare with shock, his accent thicker from adrenaline.

"He thinks you killed Megan Coldwell, his wife. The police will listen to his story, and with everything they have against you, they won't believe you. You have to kill him." My voice scratches through my tight throat. "We can frame him, Rob. You will be free. Do you understand?"

Rob stares at me. Studying me. Frightened by my words.

Willing my body to move, I stand on my weak legs. Rocking back and forth from my toes to heels, allowing my vision to go black for a moment, then sluggishly return from the outer limits of my sight. I wait for my body to gain balance, then wobble over to the large sculpture resting on the floor that Rob struck Mark with. Lifting it with haste, I struggle to balance its weight over my head. With one swift move, I drop it onto Mark's head. A dull crunch explodes from his skull, confirming my effort did the job.

"I need to clean myself up. Don't call the cops yet. We need to protect you," I say to Rob as I wobble to our bathroom, the excessive movement causing my vision to narrow again.

In our bathroom, I study myself and see my neck is red with broken flesh and my eyes bloodshot and inflamed. My neck begins to sting like thorns have woven their way into my flesh. My skin is now peppered with a mix of new and old bruises. I look like potential talent for a domestic violence poster. I have more work to do, though—only one more beating to take before I can enjoy my victory.

I quickly text Detective Cruz that I'm alone with Rob in our home and I'm scared.

I wobble back to our sitting room where Rob rests with his head between his legs. He hears my entrance and raises his head to greet me.

"Who was that, Sophia?" His voice is mystified by what he just saw me do.

"That was the husband of one of the murdered women, Megan Coldwell." I stay standing, hands in tight fists at my sides, mentally preparing for what's to come next.

"Why was he here?"

"Well, he showed up here the other night wanting to kill you for either fucking or killing his wife, maybe a little bit of both."

"But I didn't kill her."

"You fucked her, though, right?" I spit fiercely.

Silence.

He turns his head away from me.

Anger radiates from my belly and flows into my limbs.

238

"Rob." I say his name, readying myself to tell him all I've done.

He raises his eyes to meet mine as I stretch my tight neck slowly from side to side.

"You know, Sophia, the fucking nerve. I'm sick of your constant, non-stop whining. Come off it!" He stands, aggressively pointing his index finger at me and continues, "It's not as if you didn't have your fun." My brows furrow, and before I can reply, he continues, "Benjamin Booth, Sophia. You're not an innocent victim. You've had your fun, too."

I freeze. My stupid mouth left open from surprise. I thought I was so careful. I thought I planned everything so well.

"Why do you think he was fired? No, it wasn't because he was sleeping with my wife—if that's what you're thinking. I'll allow you some fun from time to time. After all, I have mine, why can't you have yours? It also wasn't the bastard baby you were carrying for ten weeks." Rob's brown eyes gleam with hatred and his upper lip slightly hooks with his words. "I fired him because he fell in love with you. He wanted what's mine and that's bad for business, Soph. You think you know him but trust me when I say that you don't. He's a worm. The type that will do anything to save his own skin," he says with a knowing smirk pulling at the corners of his mouth.

"I had you followed, Soph. That's how I confirmed it. Ben has quite a surprising past, a past that should stay clear of your future." He combs his fingers through his full dark hair and continues, "Did you know he had been under the influence while driving and caused a fatal accident? An accident where I helped him avoid legal trouble in exchange for his loyalty. Do something like that for someone, they are determined to be loyal, like a dog saved from the pound. That is until he set his eyes on your fucking face." His words sharp and purposely hurtful.

His mocking grin turns into a dazzling smile. "I know everything, Sophia."

Before fury blurs my vision, tingles my toes, and quivers my bottom lip, my stomach dives into my pelvis as I try to focus the rage on Rob's smiling face. I step closer to him, readying myself for checkmate in our little game of chess.

I'm the fucking queen.

"You don't know everything, Robert," I say, seething.

"I do, Sophia." His arrogance shines proudly through his tone.

"No, because you don't know that I went to the open house while you were in Vegas, where I fucked Jacob Hope and a woman you know named Veronica." His jaw drops open, his ego now checked. "Wait, it gets better," I say, putting my hand up with a grin plastered on my face. "I stole fentanyl from your storage, the very vial Fred warned you about. With it, I killed Megan, Brooke, Rosey, Abby, and, finally, Veronica. I left your cum at Abby's and a bottle of your wine with your fingerprints on it at Veronica's." I take a deep, overly dramatic inhale.

His body falls sluggishly back into the chair he was sitting in when I walked back in the room. His eyes stare at me.

I'm toying with him. This moment is everything I hoped it would be. Joy fills me with enthusiasm.

I lean over his hunched torso and say, "In case you don't get what I'm saying...I murdered your whores and made it look like it was you. Oh! And *that* guy on the floor," I point to Mark's lifeless body, "he figured out it was me who killed his wife. He was here to kill *me* tonight, not you!" I laugh.

I then laugh harder at the absurdity of it all and how much fun it is to finally divulge all this information to him. His eyes finally rise to meet mine, and I offer a condescending smile.

He stands quickly, striking me across the face with the back of his heavy hand.

"Finally! What took you so long?" I joke, instigating him, watching his eyes grow with panic.

Rage in his face burns it a bright red. His nostrils widen. "Why?" he says through tightly clenched teeth.

Adrenaline rushes through my veins, pushing me through the dizziness caused by his slap. "Are you fucking serious? You're not dumb. I know you're a selfish fuck who likes to screw his way through his insecurities, but you're not stupid."

He strikes me again, causing my knees to buckle as I fall to the floor. "You're lying," he roars.

"Oh, denial! That's original." I'm teasing and now genuinely laughing at him from my knees.

"I'll fucking—"

I interrupt him, "End me?" I continue mocking him, "Yeah, I've heard that before. I've also heard you say those words to Brooke in your office, while you held her against the wall by her throat."

His light brown eyes widen with surprise now mixed with rage. He hits me with a closed fist, and then again. I slowly raise my head, glancing up at him from the floor, until our eyes meet. His eyes now vacant of any emotion except pure rage. There is nothing left inside him but the need to hurt me. To make me pay. His primitive urgency to gain control extinguishes any reason.

Control—his most coveted asset—now gone.

He raises his fist and drops it onto me again and again. I hold on and take the beating as blood spills from my mouth, splashing across the white rug beneath me. The bones in my head strain frantically to be strong, to not cave to his fists. As I lay on the ground, he begins to kick me and I feel something snap in my chest.

It will all be over soon, I sooth myself. I close my eyes tightly, imagining Cassidy playing the piano after school as a little girl. Her glossy ash hair hanging past the stool as her little fingers delicately press the keys.

A loud, muffled firecracker deals one clean pop.

My mind creeps back into my body, jumbled by strange new sensations. Confusion diminishes any judgement. My body is weightless, yet I'm standing, which further confuses my already dizzy mind.

Detective Cruz is positioned defensively in front of me, her face flushed with fright. Her small mouth twisting with forceful words, a vein bulges from her forehead. Her voice muted to me as her pink lips bend slowly with each word. Her voice sounds as if it's being carried from far away. It feels as if I'm in my dream on the rooftop and the wind is drowning all sound.

Her gun is drawn and pointed at me.

My body is jerked backwards by someone holding me tightly. My legs flail, attempting to gain balance but I'm raised again by the arm squeezing painfully tight around my chest. Rob's voice is snug to my ear. His slick cheek pressed securely to mine from behind. His tight hold making it a grueling task for my lungs to fill completely with each breath.

My mind strains to place puzzle pieces of time together, but the missing pieces cannot be retrieved. Blood marinates my tongue as everything blurs in slowed time. Their voices begin to break through the silence.

Rob and Cruz are arguing. Rob's tone is combative, yet franticly desperate.

"Robert, listen to me. You don't want to do this," Cruz pleads with him, gun still pointed at us.

"I didn't do any of this. It wasn't me. It was her!" He yanks me backwards again, digging something into my throat, causing my skin to burn, followed by wet warmth dribbling down my neck.

"Robert! Put the knife down. Come on. Be smart!"

"You're not listening! She did it! She framed me. All of it. It was her!" His volume a deafening roar in my ear.

"Okay, put the knife down and we can talk. I'll listen, but I can't do anything for you while you have a knife to Sophia's throat."

"You don't believe me, do you?" He squeezes my ribs brutally tight with his arm, forcing any remaining air from my lungs, and I feel another excruciating crack from my ribs.

"Robert, just put the knife down and we can talk all you want. I want to believe you, Robert."

Everything now moves with crystal clarity instead of a confusing puzzle never to be solved. Rob moves abruptly backwards, digging the blade deeper into my neck. I whimper at the pressure and turn my head to the side. With our faces touching, I whisper his name so quietly that he listens to my words.

Detective Cruz continues negotiating with Rob as I speak to the man I loved, to the man I called my husband. He leans closer to my lips, with the knife still to my throat.

"Rob," I whisper again through the fogginess of my tight throat. "Rob, it was never going to be me," I recite the words I say aloud in my dream to him just before shoving him off the ledge, watching him tumble off the tall city building.

His voice soothes as he replies quietly to Cruz, calmly explaining that he doesn't blame her or anyone else for what they believe. He knows how it looks—how he looks. He repositions the knife to a fresh new patch of flesh on my neck.

"There's really only one thing left for me to do, then, isn't there, detective?" Rob presses down on the blade. His strength wavers as he presses as hard as his adrenaline-fatigued muscles allow, then begins to drag it across my throat. Slowly, deeply.

Another loud pop hammers off the walls of my living room. His body jolts violently. A thick, warm mist lands on my cheek as Rob's body drops to the floor, knocking me onto my hands and knees.

Looking behind me at his expressionless face, his perfect coffee-colored hair wet from the head wound Detective Cruz just delivered. His lifeless brown eyes seem to follow me as I rise to my feet.

Cruz is at him, kicking the knife away and securing the scene. She begins yelling into her phone.

I step back as my eyes take in the scene of my home's broken interior. The Claire Family Grandfather clock strikes 1:00 a.m.

as the pendulum swings. My home I tirelessly remodeled and shared with my husband now storing not one, but two corpses. My brain begins to plan the clean-up project. The powerlessness and hatred that pulsed through me floats away like a cloud of exhaled smoke.

"Sophia!" Cruz barks at me, still standing above Rob's body.

I stop planning my clean-up project and look to her as she steps towards me.

"You're bleeding," Cruz says as she applies pressure on the wound Rob left on my neck. "You're okay," she states as her eyes meet mine for a moment before they shoot back to Rob's lifeless body.

I allow Cruz to hold me as the sirens creep closer.

25

Without Notice and Quietly

Sitting on my porch, I admire the view I once shared with Rob. Watching the people of my city in the distance scurry along at tasks they find important. I'm expected to meet Ben at his apartment in an hour for drinks before we go out to dinner. He says he has a surprise for me, but I have one for him, too.

I'm floating in a moment of realization where everything feels gloriously right. I know the world is still a chaotic mess riddled with evil, but in this very moment, in this bubble of time, everything feels perfectly whole. My thumb searches for my wedding ring to spin but finds only bare skin.

It's been six months since the night Rob was shot dead in my home, and Mark was found beaten to death by Rob. The world believes Rob killed Mark, but only after Mark attempted to kill me. You see, I was supposed to be Mark's revenge. His eye for an eye for Rob killing his Megan.

I've remodeled again. It's like a new house, with a new start. Rob's body was sent home to London for his family to bury. I refused to attend the funeral of a murderer of women, naturally. Detective Cruz was praised for saving my life by national media and per procedure, she took time off after fatally shooting a civilian. We haven't spoken since that night. While she was easy to manipulate, I still find myself thinking about her occasionally. I'm confused by my genuine passion for her.

Of course, those who knew Rob said they would have never known. They all declared what a nice guy he was. That he was a good man. That he was so kind, generous, polite…blah, blah, blah. Then, there were the countless women who had affairs, or wanted to have affairs with him. Some dramatically told their story as if they were next to meet death at the hands of Robert Charles Claire, as if they were the lucky ones who escaped death.

I met with the families of the murdered women. We shared tears, sympathies, and posed for press photos. At the time, the press photos displayed my significant bruises and broken skin. I'm an extraordinary survivor to all.

I offered to reimburse all burial costs to each family, using Rob's inherited estate to do so. At first, Rob's family had threatened to step in on his estate regardless of the no-contest clause in his will and me being his trustee. However, after I explained to his mother how it would look to the press, she backed off. She—like Rob did—values image and ego above all else.

I didn't kill Rob; he did that himself. I simply used his ego against him. I manipulated him in a way that suited me.

I exploited his fear of not controlling the situation. Eventually, his intense fear sparked his imagination at the perfect moment, and he grew inconsolable at the idea of what awaited him. Detective Cruz did the rest.

To know other women experienced my husband's body the way I did was enough to break what we were. Knowing it continued to happen regularly ruined any chance of fixing us. I'm not sure I could have ever forgotten about his cheating, even if it stopped. It would have always been with us, staining each intimate moment. The thought of his mouth on lips that beg for more, his deep moans due to another woman pleasuring him, and, most of all, his joy of the hunt that gave him the ultimate high. While there was a strange pride that came with knowing I was the wife and he always came home to me, that doesn't mean that's who I wanted to be. I refuse to be that woman.

Rob twisted me into someone I didn't know, but someone who already existed inside me. I can't blame him completely; he brought out what was already there. The sleepy wolf waited to be awakened, then disappeared when he did, leaving a newly formed person in its place. This person I am now, this new version of me, I'm still getting acquainted with her.

Ben fights every day to be in my life and his mind cannot understand why I won't allow him to slide into the position Rob had held. He doesn't understand why he isn't sleeping next to me each night and waking up to me each morning. Our pillow talk had always circled back to that one topic; us being together if Rob wasn't in the picture.

He had appeared routinely in my life after the night Rob and Mark died in my home, wanting to be the lighthouse in my storm. I kept him away by being too busy with all that happens after such events. I still see him casually…when I'm not with Viktor.

He has yet to find out about Viktor, but I don't think he'll have a chance to.

I met Viktor at an event for Anexa a few years ago. He is a gentleman who owns a rather large securities company in Russia. He is quiet, confident, and has a stoic attitude I admire. He isn't flashy, spoiled, or egotistical like Robert Charles Claire was. He doesn't need to lie like Ben to have a woman love him. Viktor's quiet conviction can be felt by those near him. He doesn't have to reiterate his status to others to be validated. His directness is what captivated me. I've been around Rob, someone who manipulated each situation with treachery and misrepresentations for so long that hearing the truth is like feeling the warmth of the sun.

When does love die, exactly? Well, Rob never loved me. Not like I loved him. Neither did Ben; someone who loves another doesn't keep a secret of that magnitude from their true love. Both were enamored with me and that is superficial, even though it can imitate love, but it lives a shorter life.

Just like mine and Rob's children would have been, I was a box to check off and a pretty face to fill a frame. Maybe I expected too much. Maybe it's my fault. But I thought what most women think: if I loved Rob how I wanted to be loved, he would learn to love me and give me what I needed in return. But people don't really change. Not at their core. That remains.

My cellphone alerts me to a text. I lift it and see Ben's name. He says he's home early and that I can head his way anytime. A single text from Ben had once thrilled me. It had once filled by belly with butterflies that forced a smile to tighten my lips. Now, there's nothing left but the sad memory of what could have been if he was the man with integrity I had once thought him to be.

I slip on my green Christian Louboutin alligator pumps, then head for the garage where my new car waits, but not forgetting what's left of the vial I stole from Anexa.

So, how does love die? Love dies just like Rob's victims did, without notice and quietly.

About the Author

Erica Blaque was born in Seattle, Washington where she spent her childhood taking dance and theater classes, swimming, or fearlessly forging new paths in the woods behind her parents' home. She holds a degree in business management and is constantly pursuing growth through education and trying new things, considering herself a forever student.

Greatly influenced by high-profile true crime and dark romance, Erica's novelistic style features sharp and sinister themes. She finds inspiration in the clandestine and the fearlessly authentic, as well as the humor in life's strangeness. If she isn't writing or spending time with her favorite humans, you'll find her at home reading, meditating, or binge-watching her latest Netflix obsession.